S0-EBA-008

2, 5

. 5

E.M. JOHNSON ELEM. LIBRARY
WASHOE COUNTY SCHOOL DISTRICT
GERLACH NEVADA

A Perfect Fit

by Chris "Elio" Eliopoulos

STONE ARCH BOOKS
A CAPSTONE IMPRINT

Copyright © 2013 by Chris Eliopoulos

Mr. Puzzle is published by Stone Arch Books,
a Capstone imprint
1710 Roe Crest Drive
North Mankato, Minnesota 56003
www.capstonepub.com

All rights reserved. No part of this
publication may be reproduced in whole or
in part, or stored in a retrieval system, or
transmitted in any form or by any means,
electronic, mechanical, photocopying,
recording, or otherwise, without written
permission of the publisher.

Cataloging-in-Publication Data is available
on the Library of Congress website.

ISBN (library binding): 978-1-4342-6024-6

Ashley C. Andersen Zantop - PUBLISHER
Donald Lemke - EDITOR
Michael Dahl - EDITORIAL DIRECTOR
Brann Garvey - SENIOR DESIGNER
Heather Kindseth - CREATIVE DIRECTOR
Bob Lentz - ART DIRECTOR

Printed in China by Nordica.
0413/CA21300512
032013   007226NORDF13

A Perfect Fit

BY CHRIS "ELIO" ELIOPOULOS

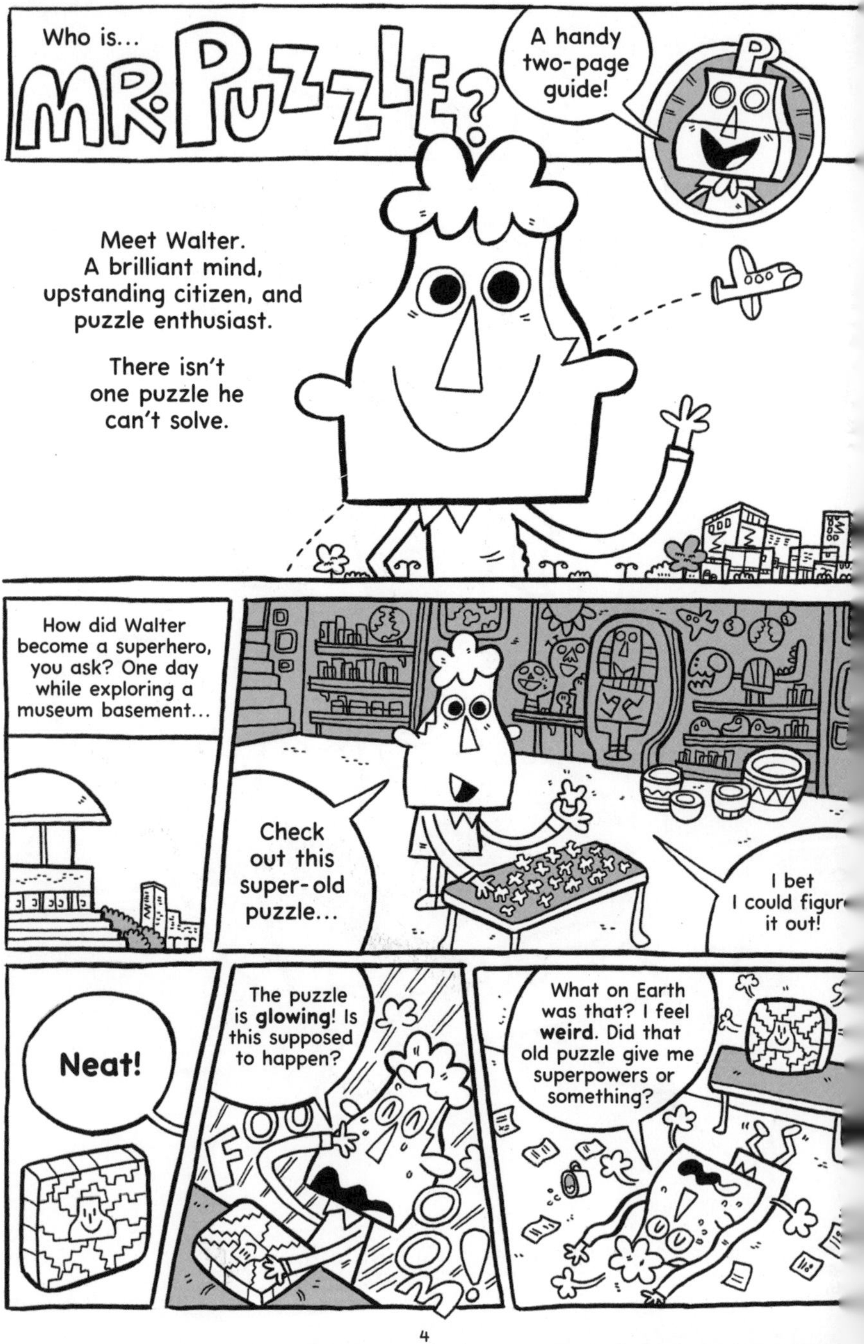
Who is...
MR. PUZZLE?
A handy two-page guide!
Meet Walter. A brilliant mind, upstanding citizen, and puzzle enthusiast.
There isn't one puzzle he can't solve.
How did Walter become a superhero, you ask? One day while exploring a museum basement...
Check out this super-old puzzle...
I bet I could figur it out!
Neat!
The puzzle is **glowing**! Is this supposed to happen?
FOOOOM!
What on Earth was that? I feel **weird**. Did that old puzzle give me superpowers or something?

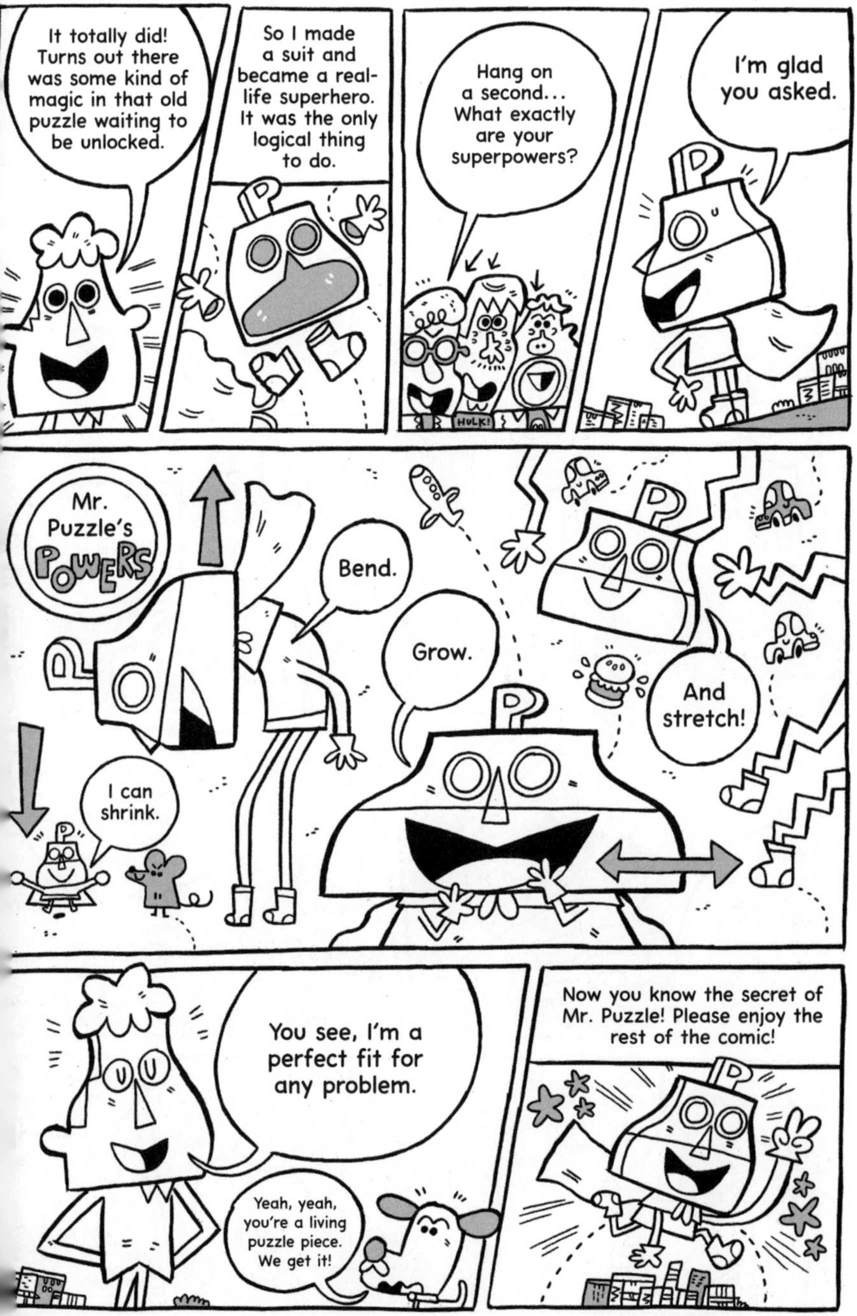
It totally did! Turns out there was some kind of magic in that old puzzle waiting to be unlocked.
So I made a suit and became a real-life superhero. It was the only logical thing to do.
Hang on a second... What exactly are your superpowers?
HULK!
I'm glad you asked.
Mr. Puzzle's POWERS
Bend.
Grow.
And stretch!
I can shrink.
You see, I'm a perfect fit for any problem.
Yeah, yeah, you're a living puzzle piece. We get it!
Now you know the secret of Mr. Puzzle! Please enjoy the rest of the comic!

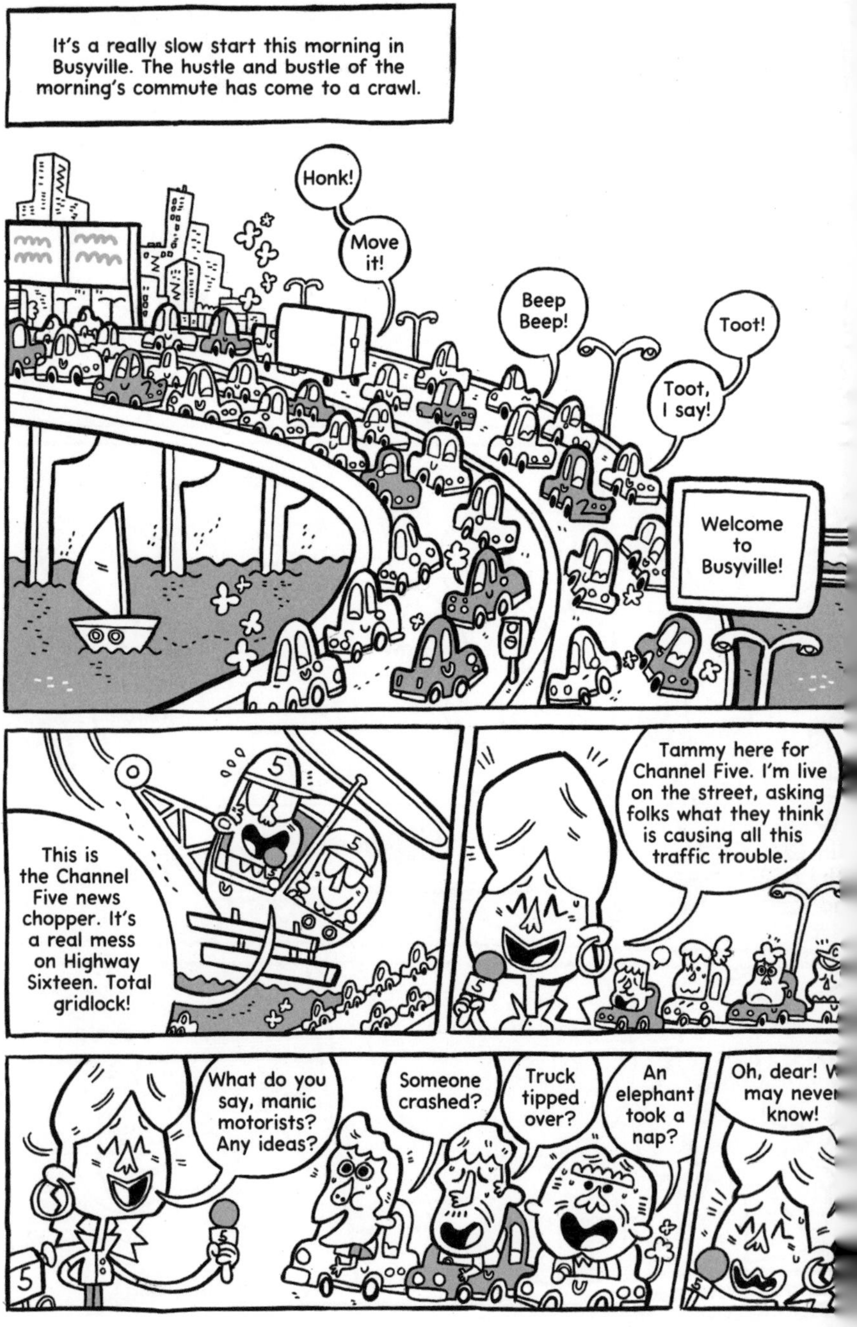
It's a really slow start this morning in Busyville. The hustle and bustle of the morning's commute has come to a crawl.
Honk!
Move it!
Beep Beep!
Toot, I say!
Toot!
Welcome to Busyville!
This is the Channel Five news chopper. It's a real mess on Highway Sixteen. Total gridlock!
Tammy here for Channel Five. I'm live on the street, asking folks what they think is causing all this traffic trouble.
What do you say, manic motorists? Any ideas?
Someone crashed?
Truck tipped over?
An elephant took a nap?
Oh, dear! W may never know!

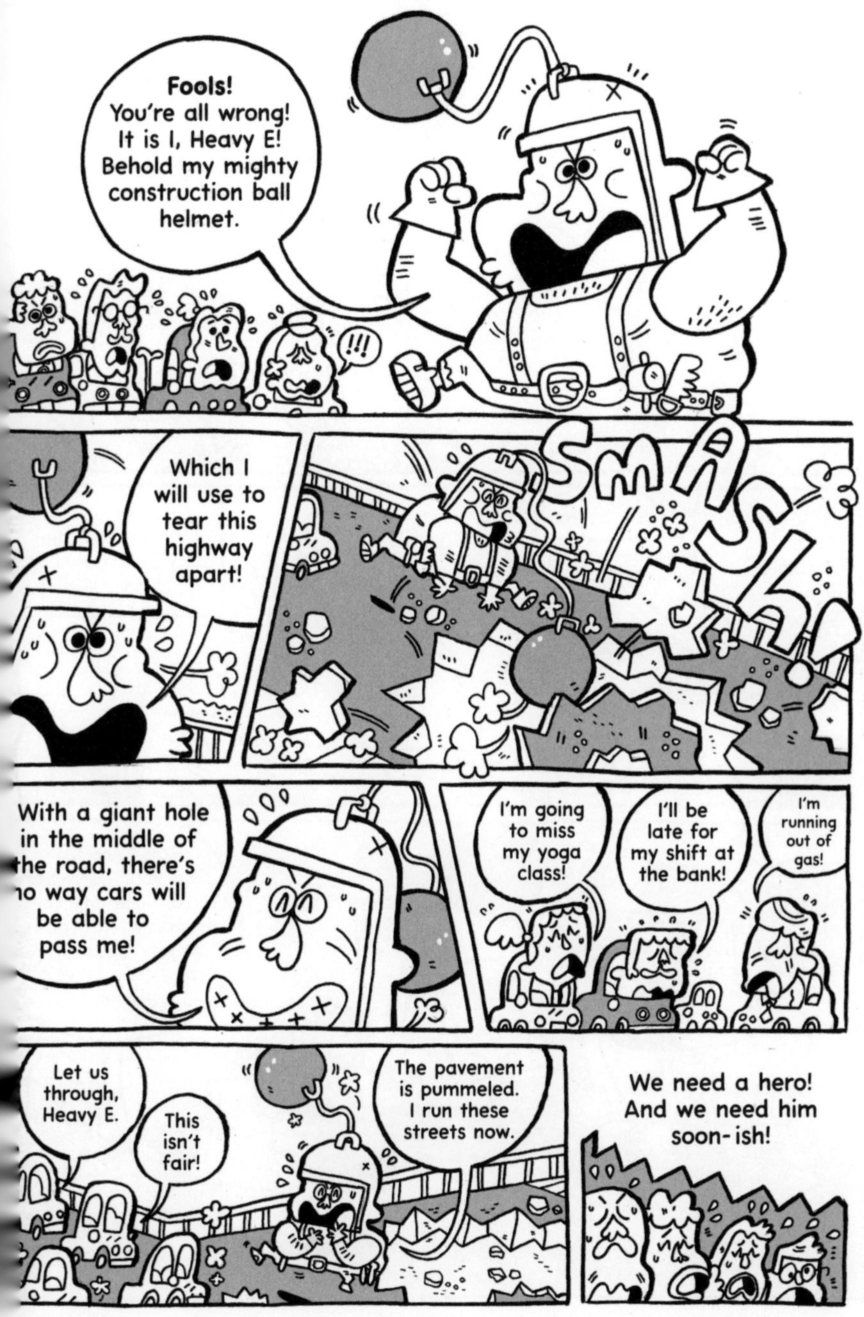
Fools! You're all wrong! It is I, Heavy E! Behold my mighty construction ball helmet.
!!!
Which I will use to tear this highway apart!
SMASH!
With a giant hole in the middle of the road, there's no way cars will be able to pass me!
I'm going to miss my yoga class!
I'll be late for my shift at the bank!
I'm running out of gas!
Let us through, Heavy E.
This isn't fair!
The pavement is pummeled. I run these streets now.
We need a hero! And we need him soon-ish!

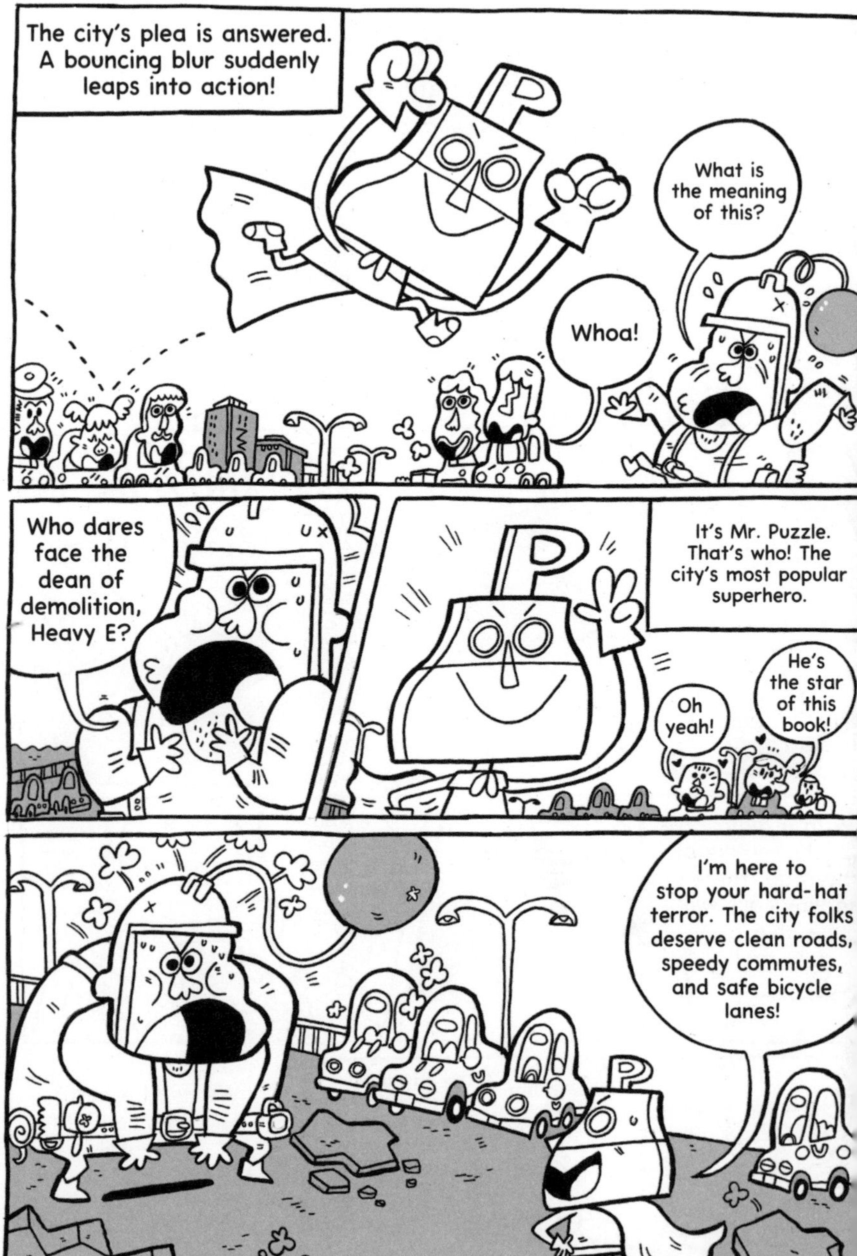
The city's plea is answered. A bouncing blur suddenly leaps into action!
What is the meaning of this?
Whoa!
Who dares face the dean of demolition, Heavy E?
It's Mr. Puzzle. That's who! The city's most popular superhero.
Oh yeah!
He's the star of this book!
I'm here to stop your hard-hat terror. The city folks deserve clean roads, speedy commutes, and safe bicycle lanes!

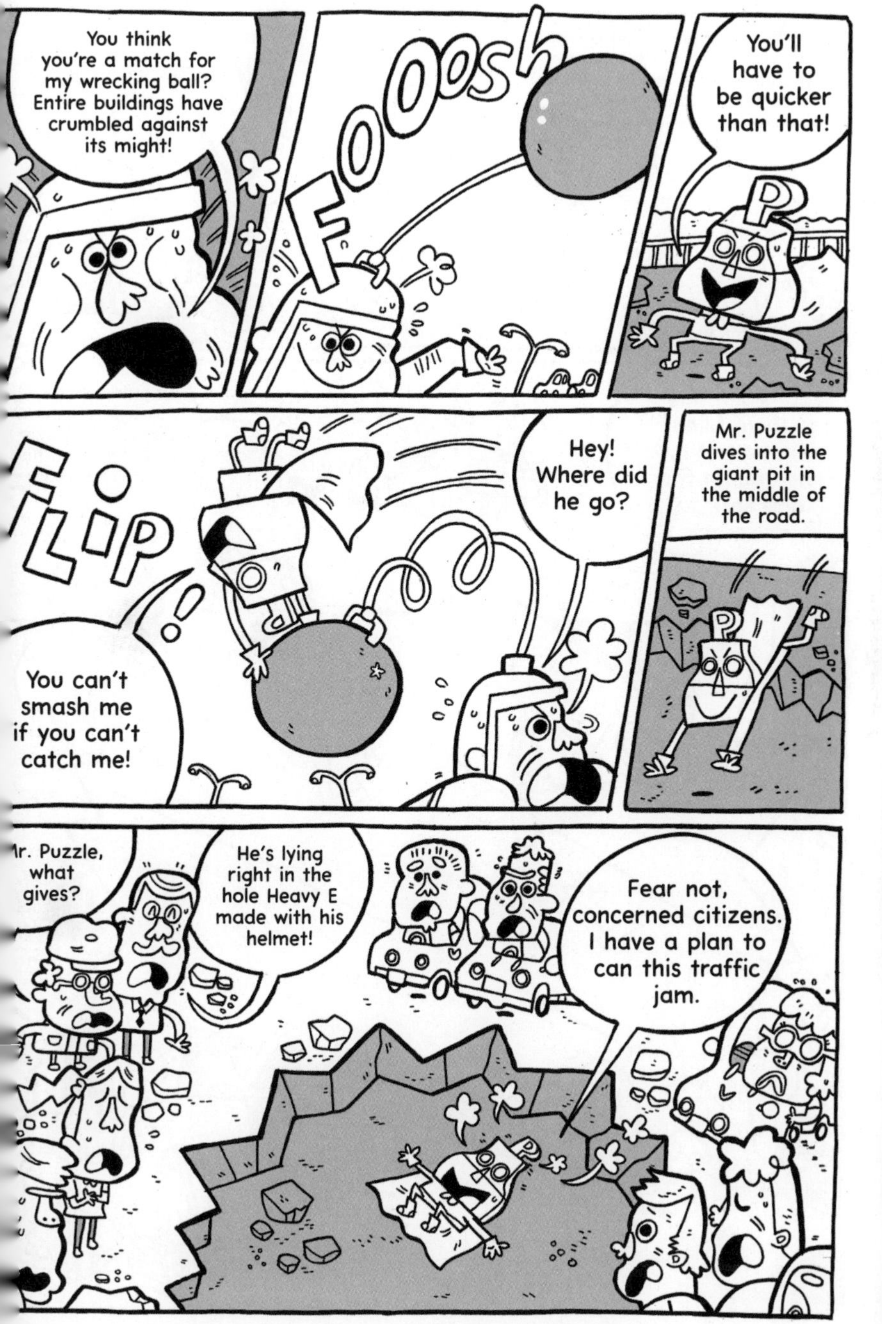

You think you're a match for my wrecking ball? Entire buildings have crumbled against its might!
FOOOOSH
You'll have to be quicker than that!
FLIP
Hey! Where did he go?
You can't smash me if you can't catch me!
Mr. Puzzle dives into the giant pit in the middle of the road.
Mr. Puzzle, what gives?
He's lying right in the hole Heavy E made with his helmet!
Fear not, concerned citizens. I have a plan to can this traffic jam.

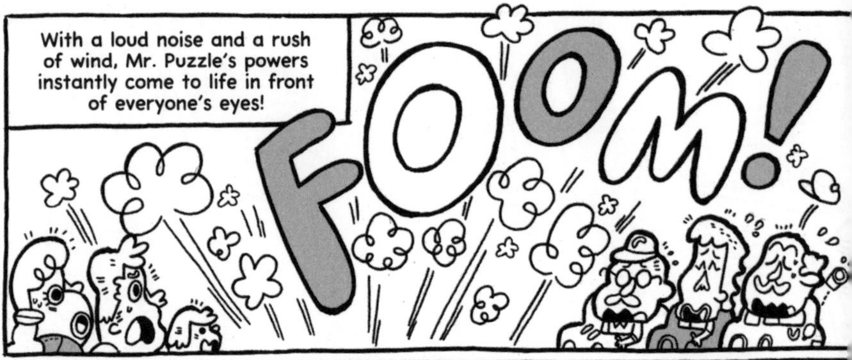
With a loud noise and a rush of wind, Mr. Puzzle's powers instantly come to life in front of everyone's eyes!
FOOM!

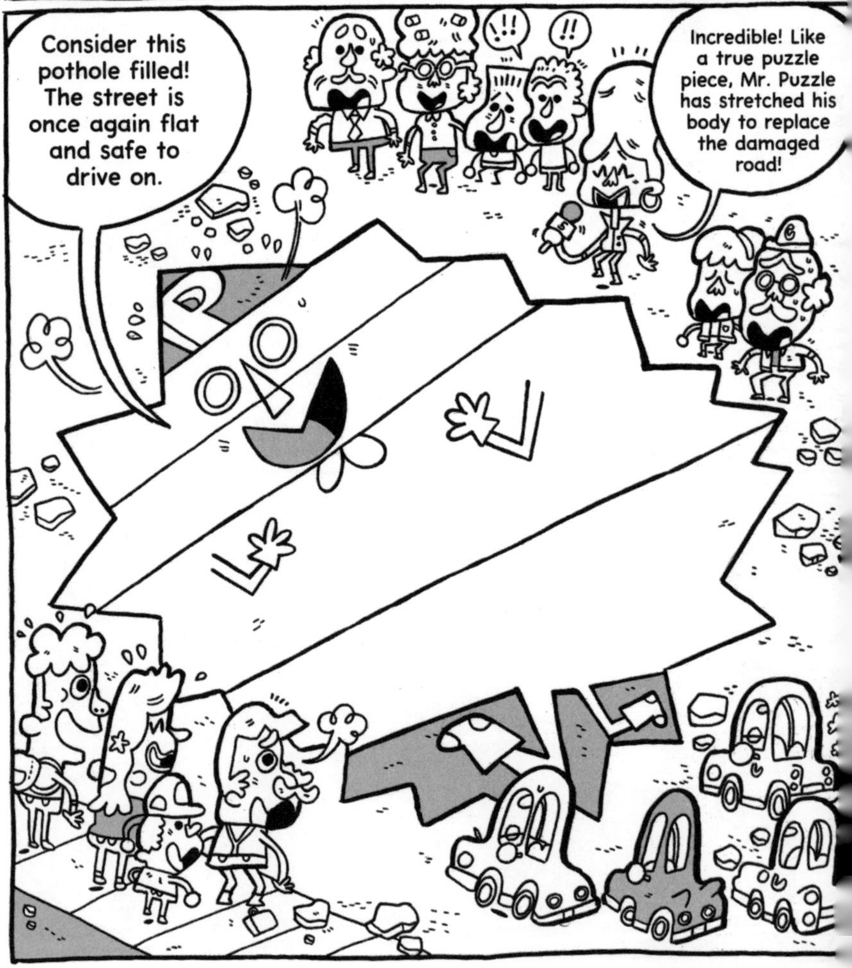
Consider this pothole filled! The street is once again flat and safe to drive on.
!!!
!!
Incredible! Like a true puzzle piece, Mr. Puzzle has stretched his body to replace the damaged road!

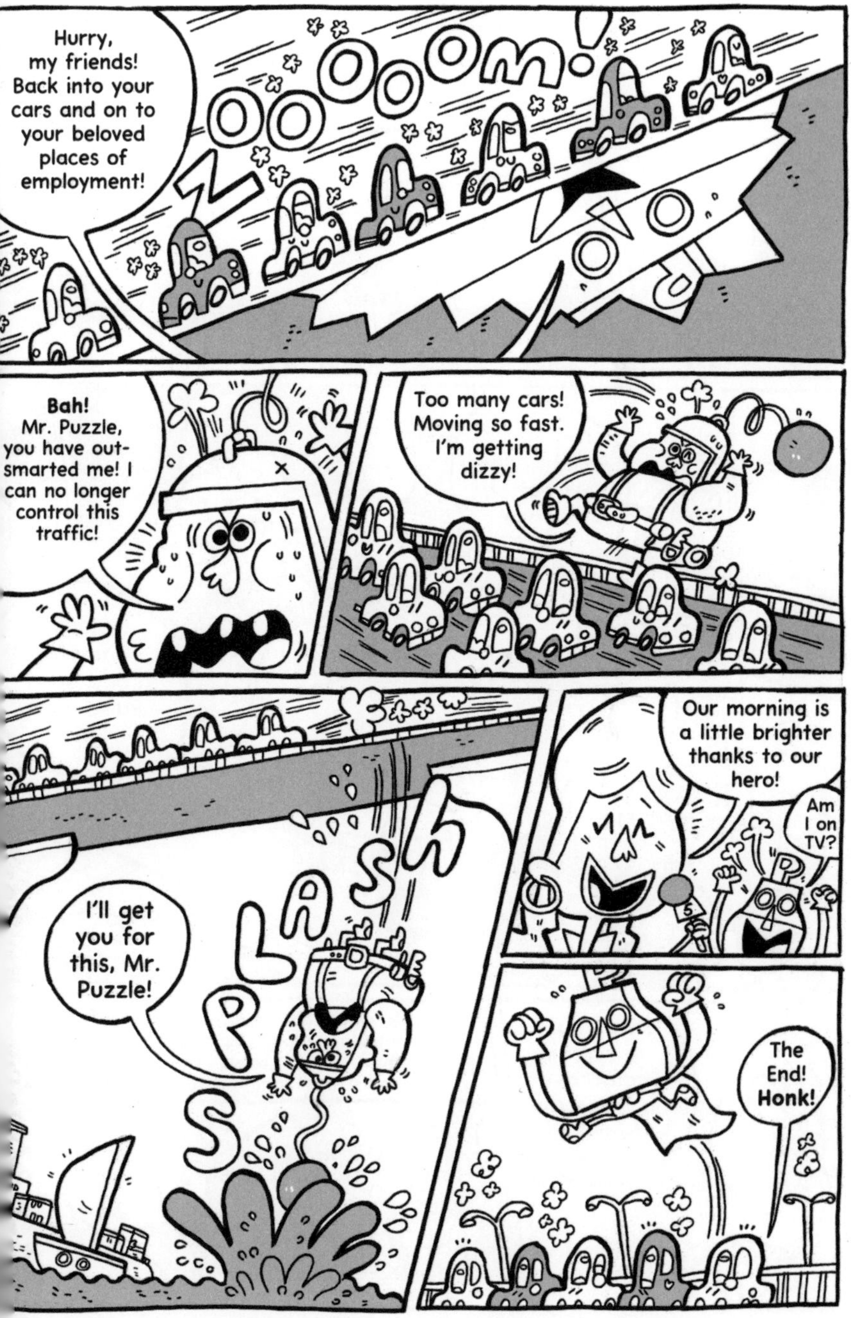

Hurry, my friends! Back into your cars and on to your beloved places of employment!
ZOOOOOOM!
Bah! Mr. Puzzle, you have out-smarted me! I can no longer control this traffic!
Too many cars! Moving so fast. I'm getting dizzy!
SPLASH
I'll get you for this, Mr. Puzzle!
Our morning is a little brighter thanks to our hero!
Am I on TV?
The End! **Honk!**

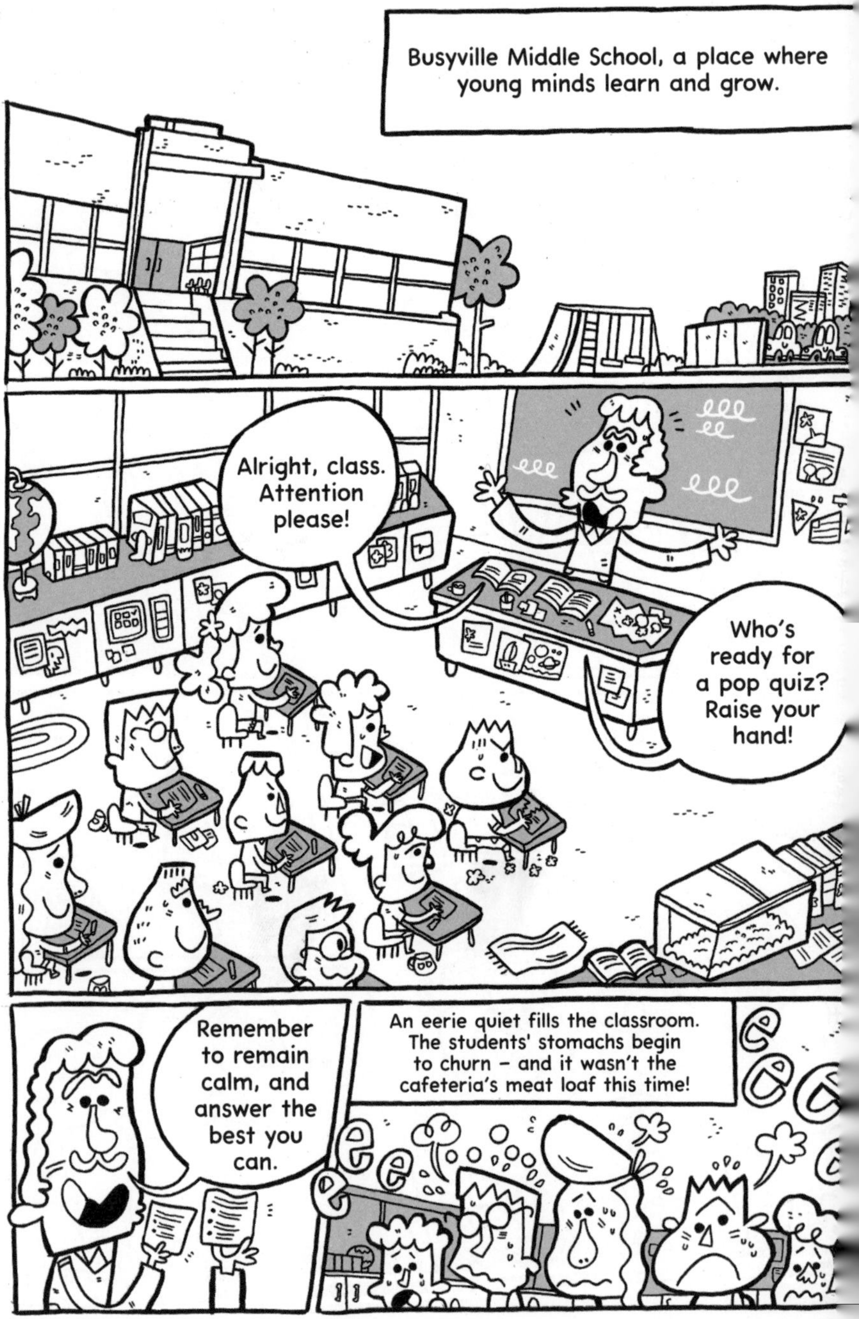

Busyville Middle School, a place where young minds learn and grow.
Alright, class. Attention please!
Who's ready for a pop quiz? Raise your hand!
Remember to remain calm, and answer the best you can.
An eerie quiet fills the classroom. The students' stomachs begin to churn – and it wasn't the cafeteria's meat loaf this time!

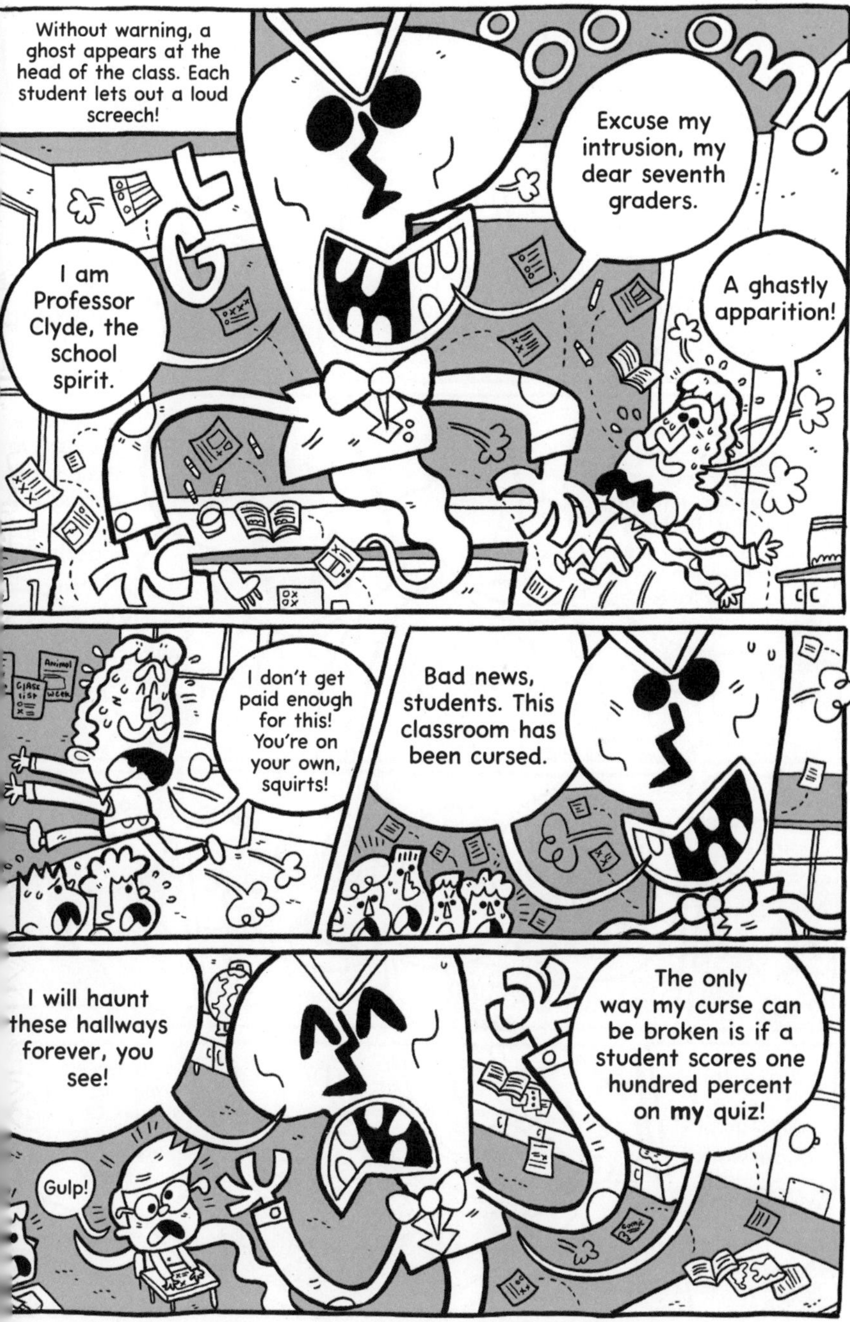
Without warning, a ghost appears at the head of the class. Each student lets out a loud screech!
OOOOOM!!
Excuse my intrusion, my dear seventh graders.
I am Professor Clyde, the school spirit.
A ghastly apparition!
I don't get paid enough for this! You're on your own, squirts!
Bad news, students. This classroom has been cursed.
I will haunt these hallways forever, you see!
The only way my curse can be broken is if a student scores one hundred percent on **my** quiz!
Gulp!

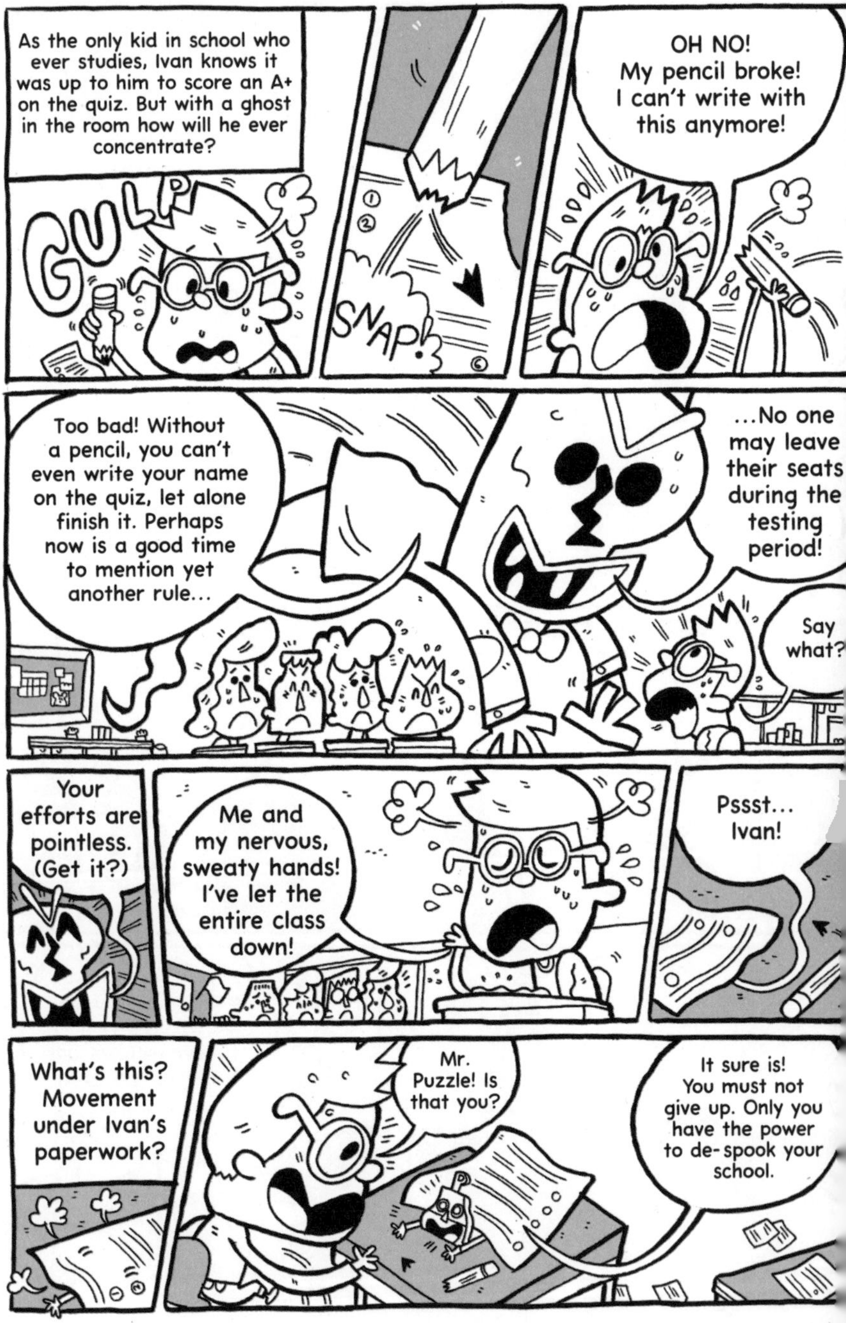
As the only kid in school who ever studies, Ivan knows it was up to him to score an A+ on the quiz. But with a ghost in the room how will he ever concentrate?
GULP
SNAP!
OH NO! My pencil broke! I can't write with this anymore!
Too bad! Without a pencil, you can't even write your name on the quiz, let alone finish it. Perhaps now is a good time to mention yet another rule...
...No one may leave their seats during the testing period!
Say what?
Your efforts are pointless. (Get it?)
Me and my nervous, sweaty hands! I've let the entire class down!
Pssst... Ivan!
What's this? Movement under Ivan's paperwork?
Mr. Puzzle! Is that you?
It sure is! You must not give up. Only you have the power to de-spook your school.

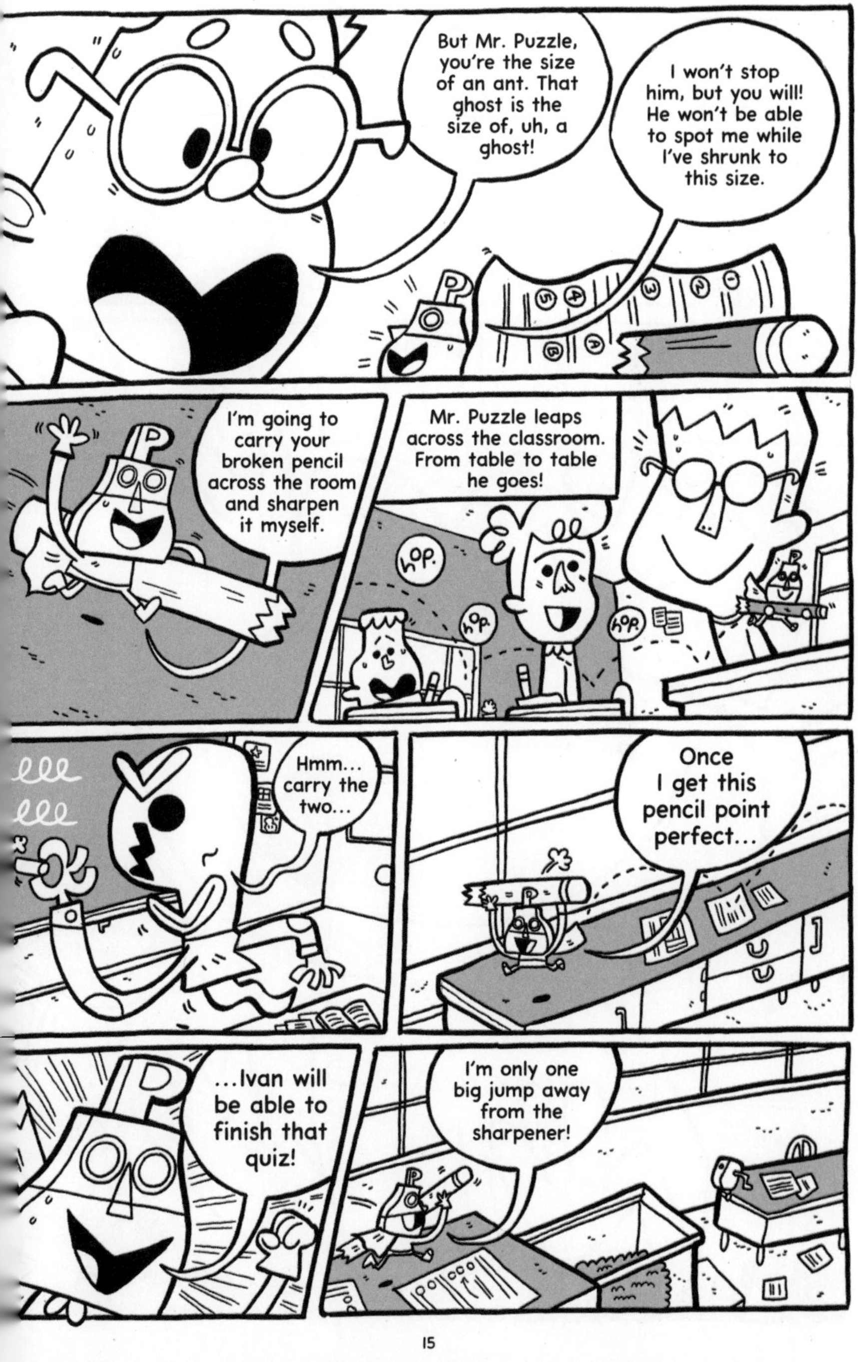
But Mr. Puzzle, you're the size of an ant. That ghost is the size of, uh, a ghost!
I won't stop him, but you will! He won't be able to spot me while I've shrunk to this size.
I'm going to carry your broken pencil across the room and sharpen it myself.
Mr. Puzzle leaps across the classroom. From table to table he goes!
hop.
hop.
hop.
Hmm... carry the two...
Once I get this pencil point perfect...
...Ivan will be able to finish that quiz!
I'm only one big jump away from the sharpener!

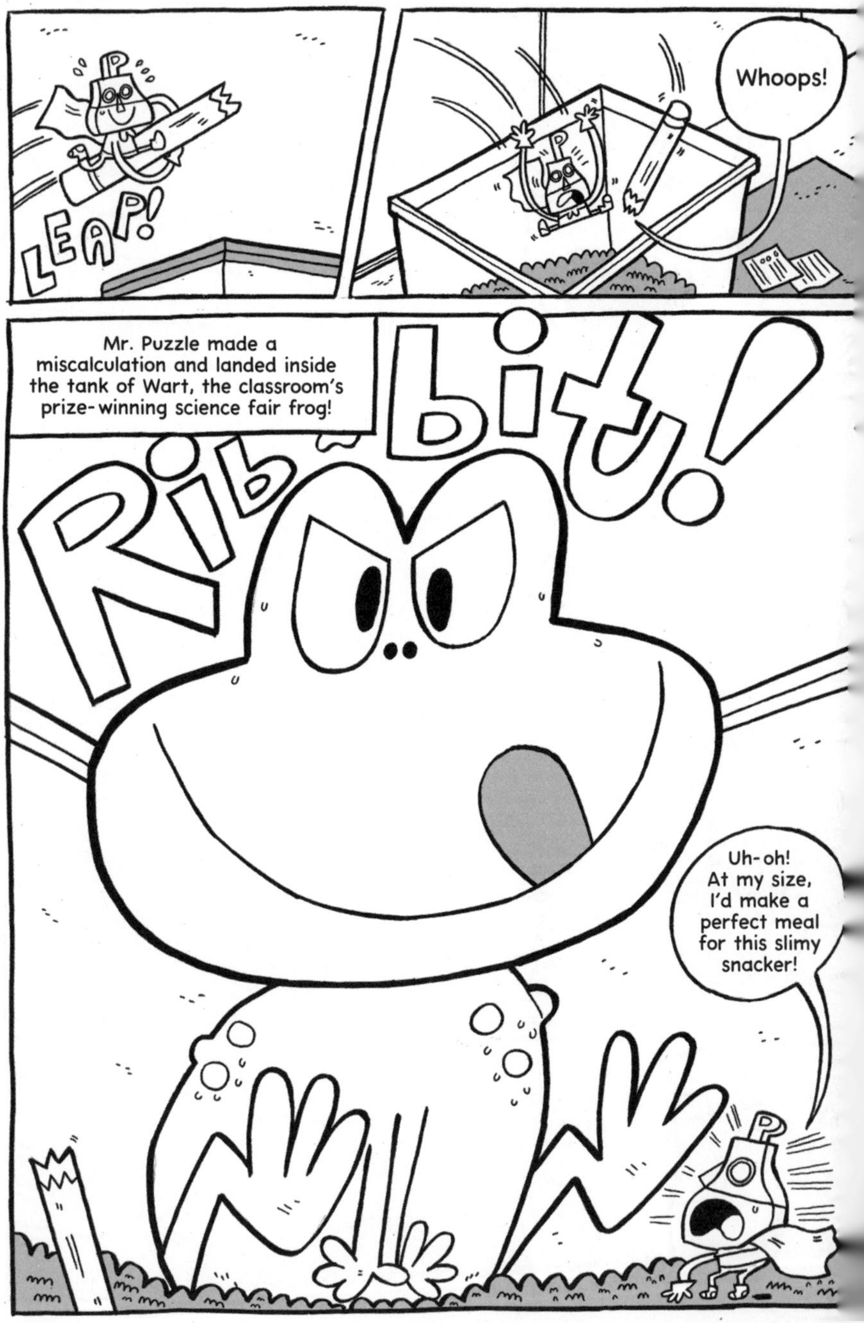
LEAP!
Whoops!
Mr. Puzzle made a miscalculation and landed inside the tank of Wart, the classroom's prize-winning science fair frog!
Ribbit!
Uh-oh! At my size, I'd make a perfect meal for this slimy snacker!

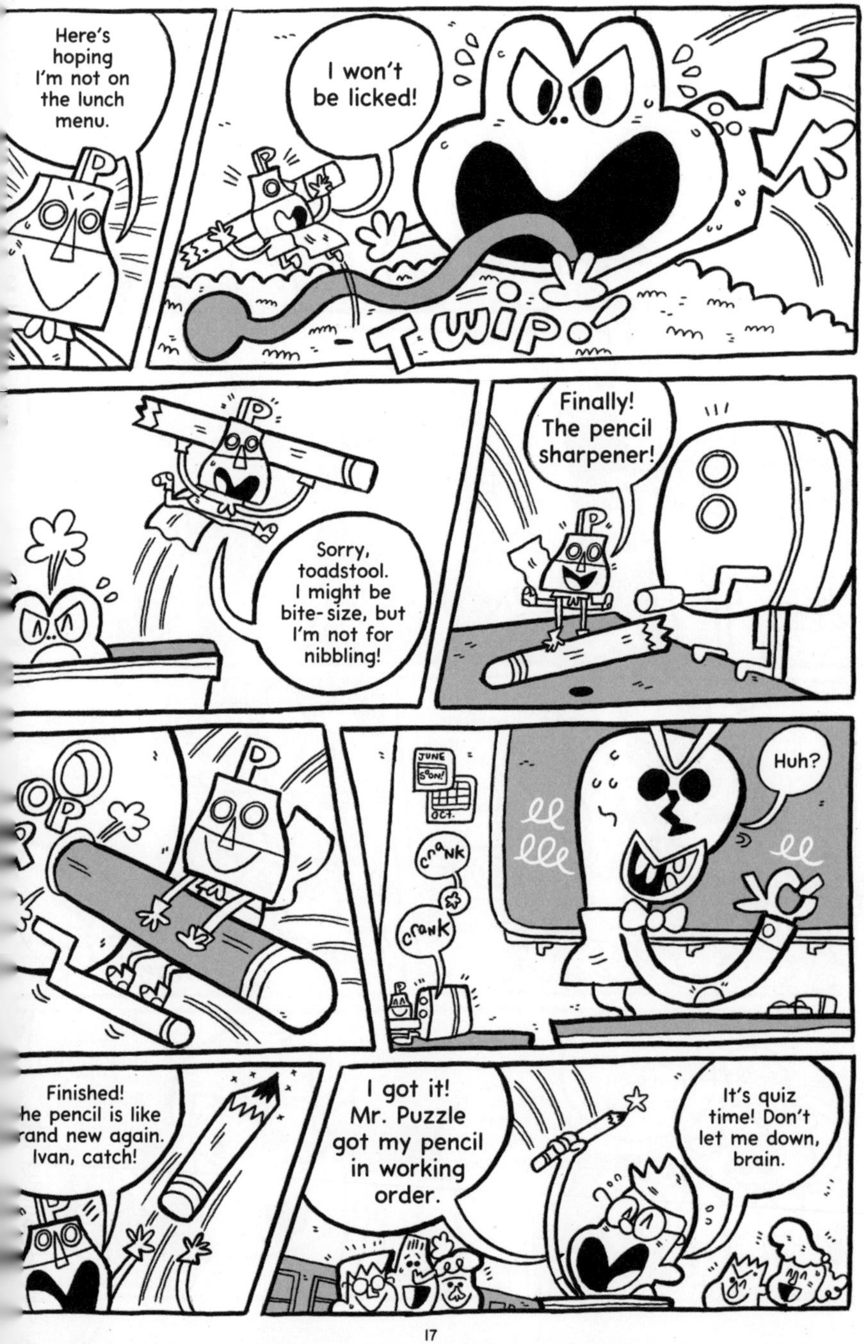
Here's hoping I'm not on the lunch menu.
I won't be licked!
TWIP!
Sorry, toadstool. I might be bite-size, but I'm not for nibbling!
Finally! The pencil sharpener!
JUNE
SOON!
OCT.
CRANK
CRANK
Huh?
Finished! he pencil is like rand new again. Ivan, catch!
I got it! Mr. Puzzle got my pencil in working order.
It's quiz time! Don't let me down, brain.

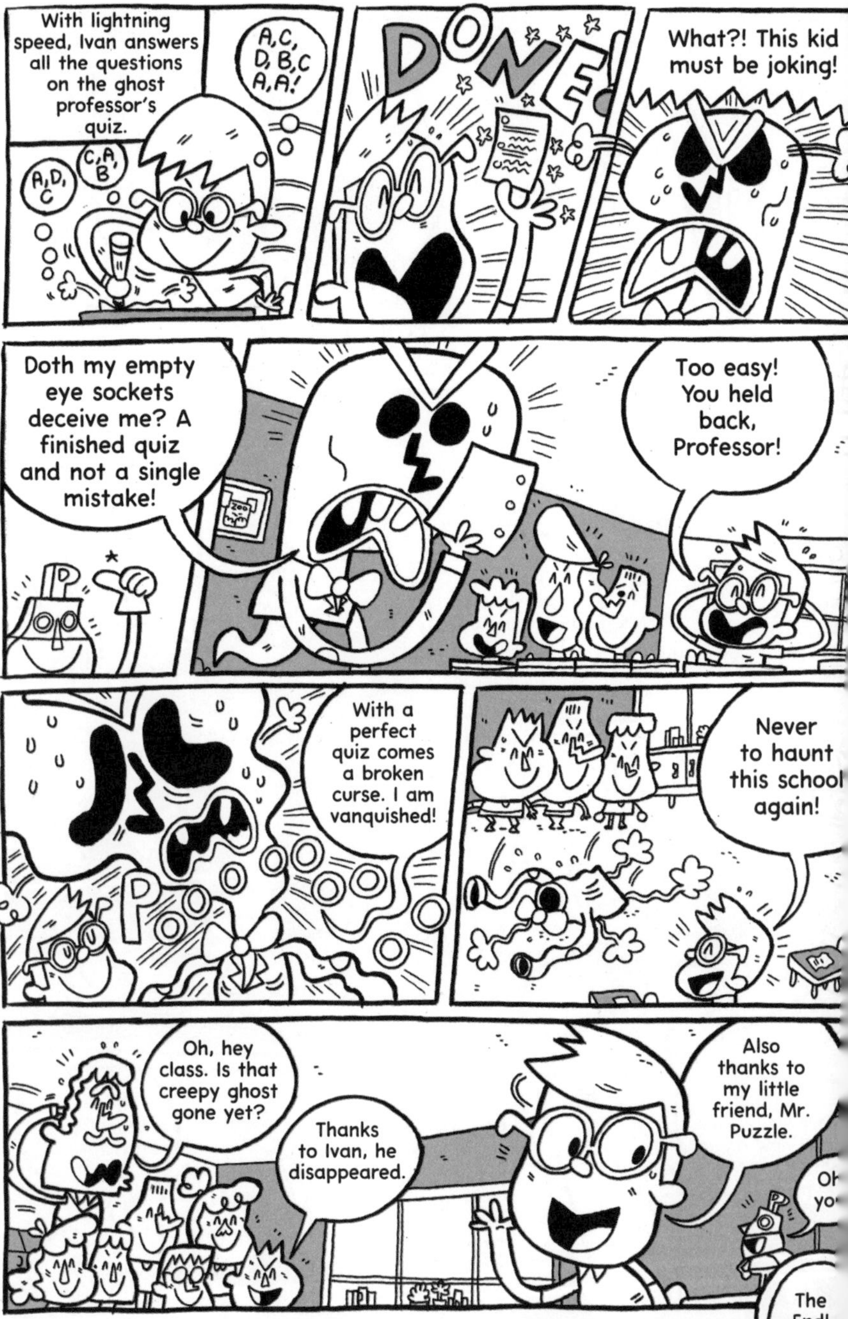

With lightning speed, Ivan answers all the questions on the ghost professor's quiz.
A,C, D,B,C A,A!
C,A, B
A,D, C
DONE!
What?! This kid must be joking!
Doth my empty eye sockets deceive me? A finished quiz and not a single mistake!
P
ZOO
Too easy! You held back, Professor!
With a perfect quiz comes a broken curse. I am vanquished!
POOOO
Never to haunt this school again!
Oh, hey class. Is that creepy ghost gone yet?
Thanks to Ivan, he disappeared.
Also thanks to my little friend, Mr. Puzzle.
The End!

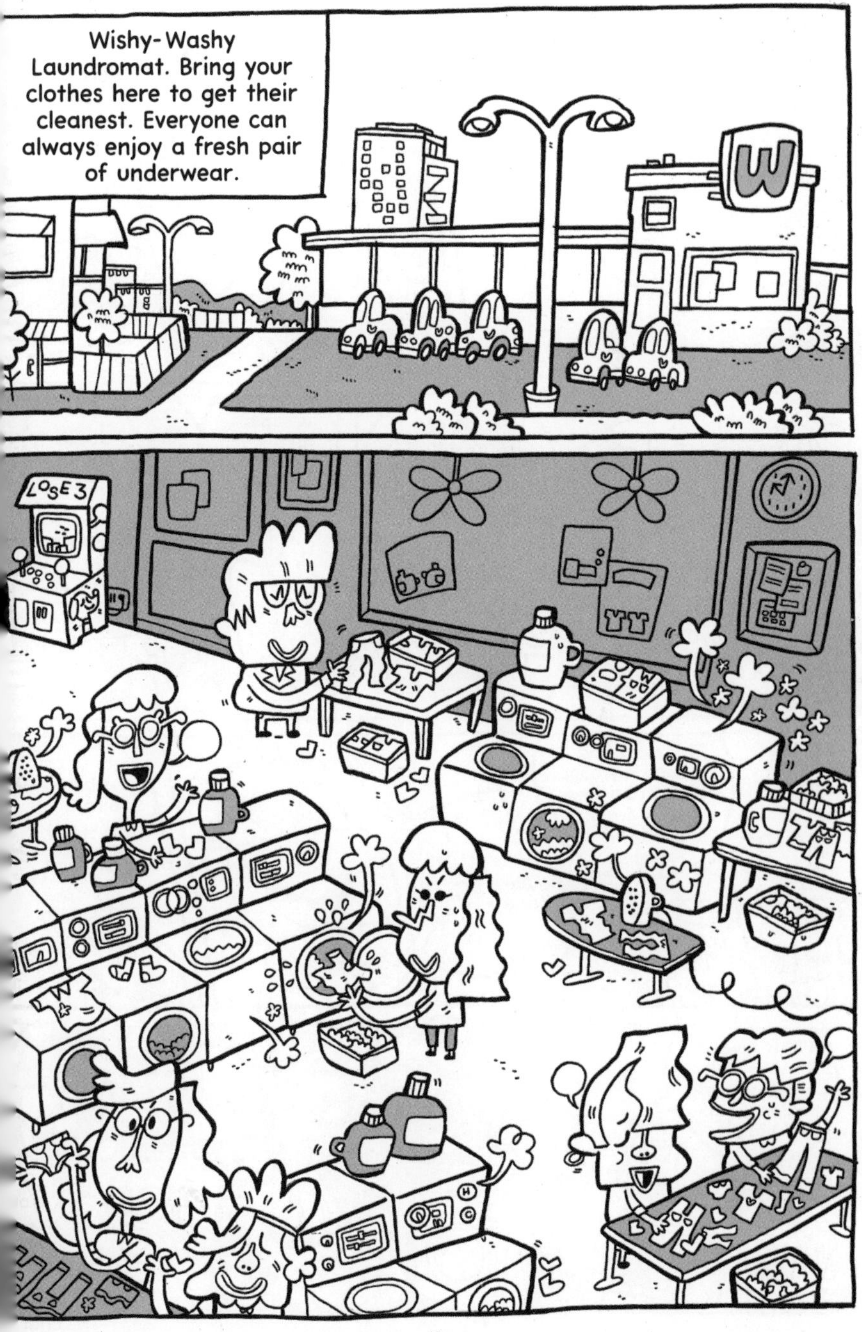
Wishy-Washy Laundromat. Bring your clothes here to get their cleanest. Everyone can always enjoy a fresh pair of underwear.
W
LOSE 3

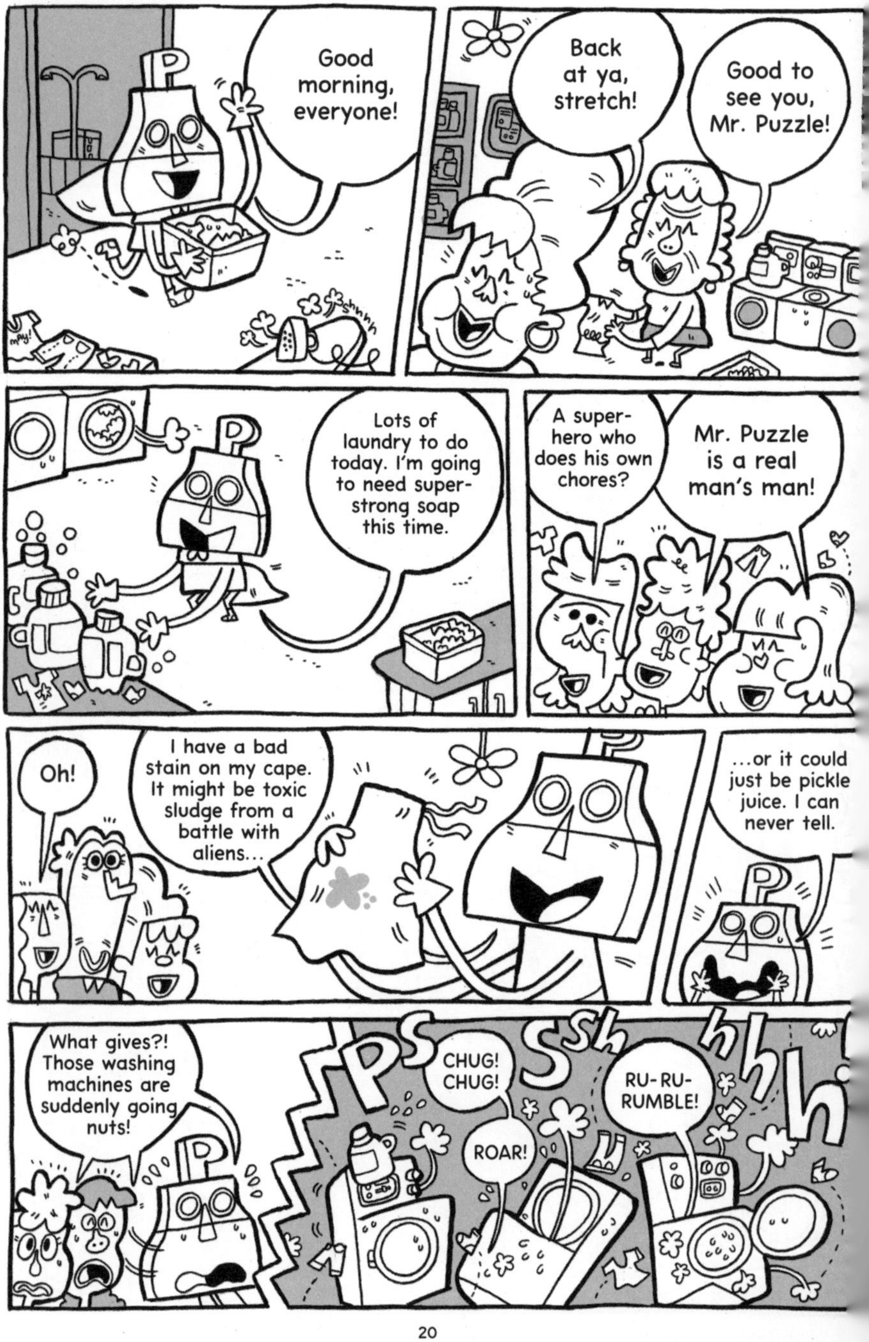
Good morning, everyone!
Back at ya, stretch!
Good to see you, Mr. Puzzle!
Lots of laundry to do today. I'm going to need super-strong soap this time.
A super-hero who does his own chores?
Mr. Puzzle is a real man's man!
Oh!
I have a bad stain on my cape. It might be toxic sludge from a battle with aliens...
...or it could just be pickle juice. I can never tell.
What gives?! Those washing machines are suddenly going nuts!
PSSShhhh
CHUG! CHUG!
ROAR!
RU-RU-RUMBLE!

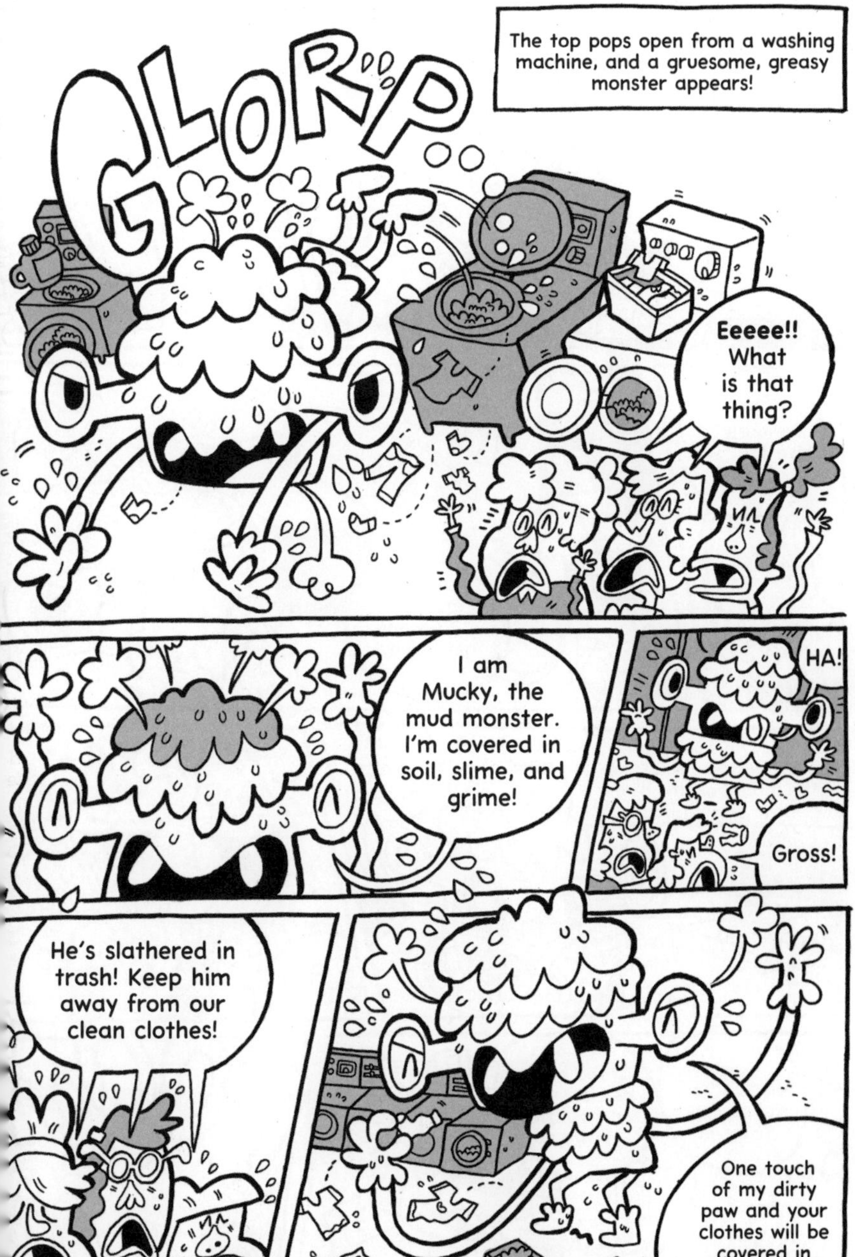
The top pops open from a washing machine, and a gruesome, greasy monster appears!
GLORP
Eeeee!! What is that thing?
I am Mucky, the mud monster. I'm covered in soil, slime, and grime!
HA!
Gross!
He's slathered in trash! Keep him away from our clean clothes!
One touch of my dirty paw and your clothes will be covered in grass stains.

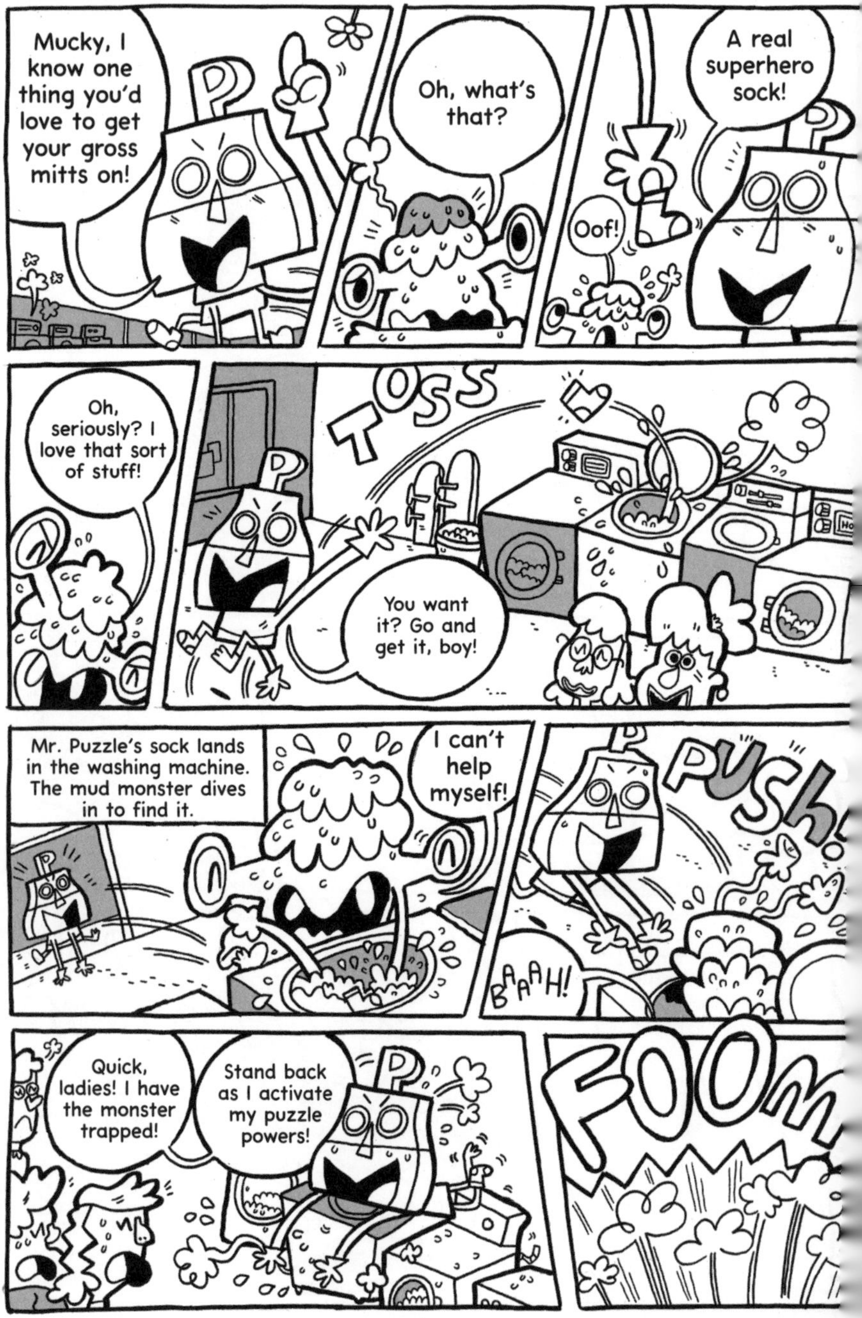
Mucky, I know one thing you'd love to get your gross mitts on!
Oh, what's that?
A real superhero sock!
Oof!
Oh, seriously? I love that sort of stuff!
TOSS
You want it? Go and get it, boy!
Mr. Puzzle's sock lands in the washing machine. The mud monster dives in to find it.
I can't help myself!
PUSH!
BAAAH!
Quick, ladies! I have the monster trapped!
Stand back as I activate my puzzle powers!
FOOM

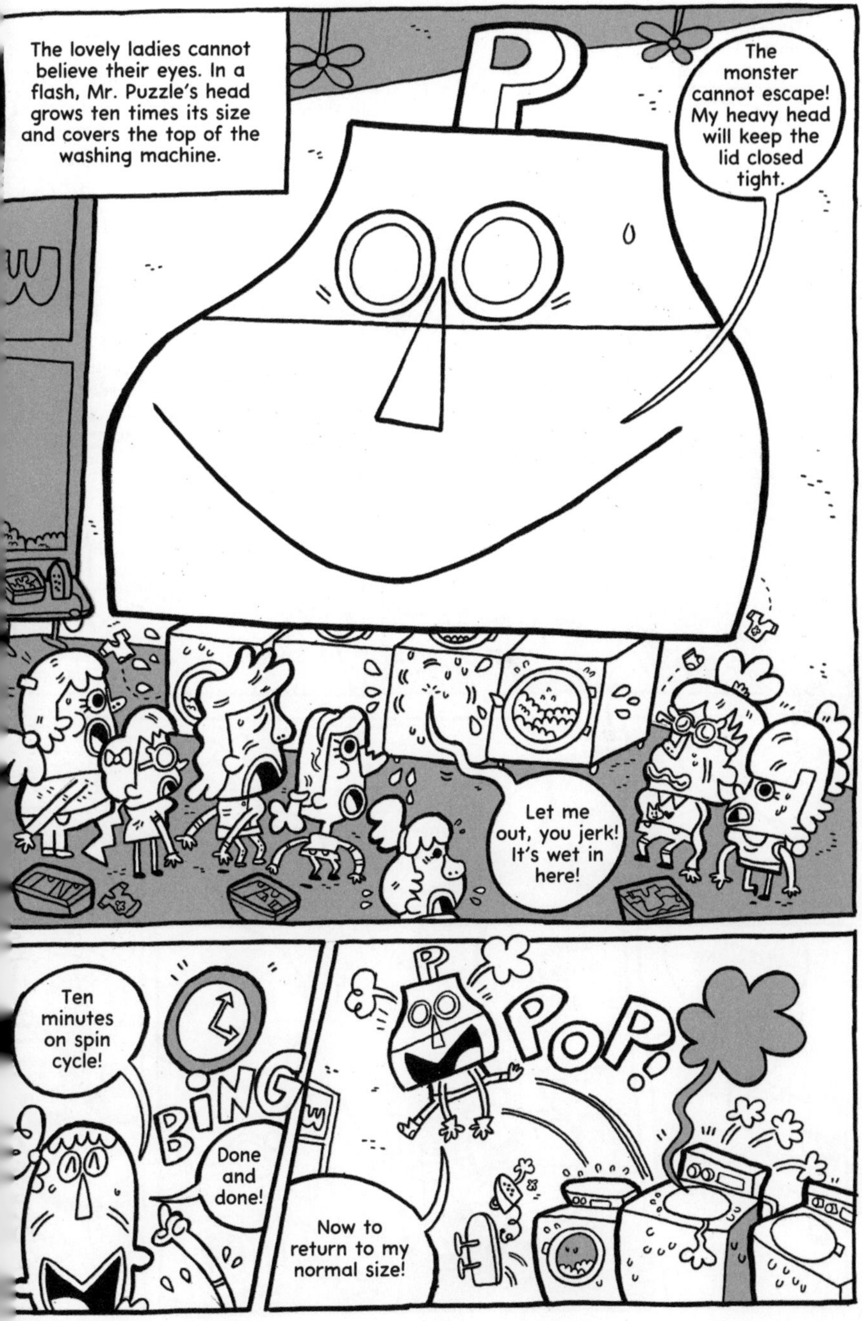
The lovely ladies cannot believe their eyes. In a flash, Mr. Puzzle's head grows ten times its size and covers the top of the washing machine.
The monster cannot escape! My heavy head will keep the lid closed tight.
Let me out, you jerk! It's wet in here!
Ten minutes on spin cycle!
BING
Done and done!
Now to return to my normal size!
POP!

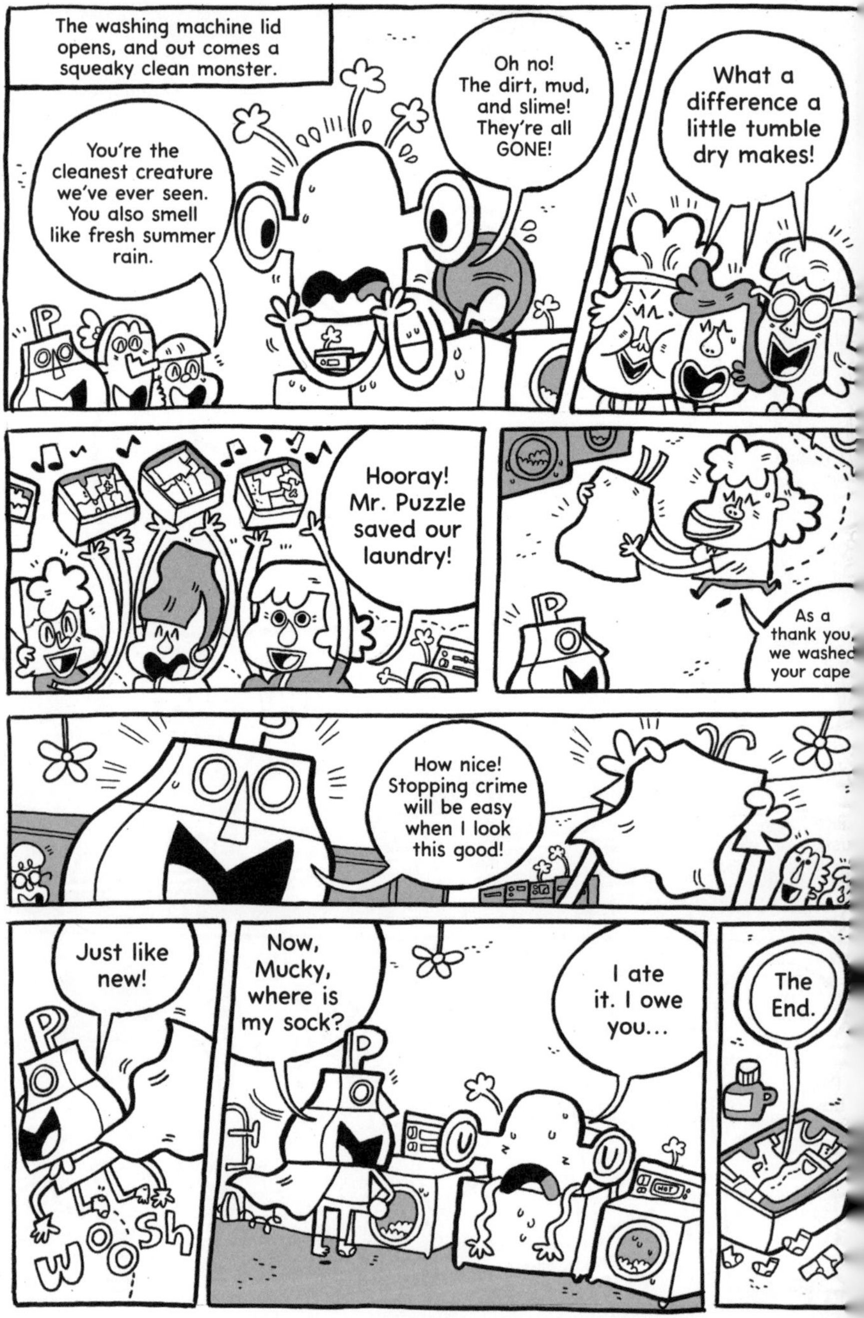

The washing machine lid opens, and out comes a squeaky clean monster.
You're the cleanest creature we've ever seen. You also smell like fresh summer rain.
Oh no! The dirt, mud, and slime! They're all GONE!
What a difference a little tumble dry makes!
Hooray! Mr. Puzzle saved our laundry!
As a thank you, we washed your cape
How nice! Stopping crime will be easy when I look this good!
Just like new!
WOOSh
Now, Mucky, where is my sock?
I ate it. I owe you...
The End.

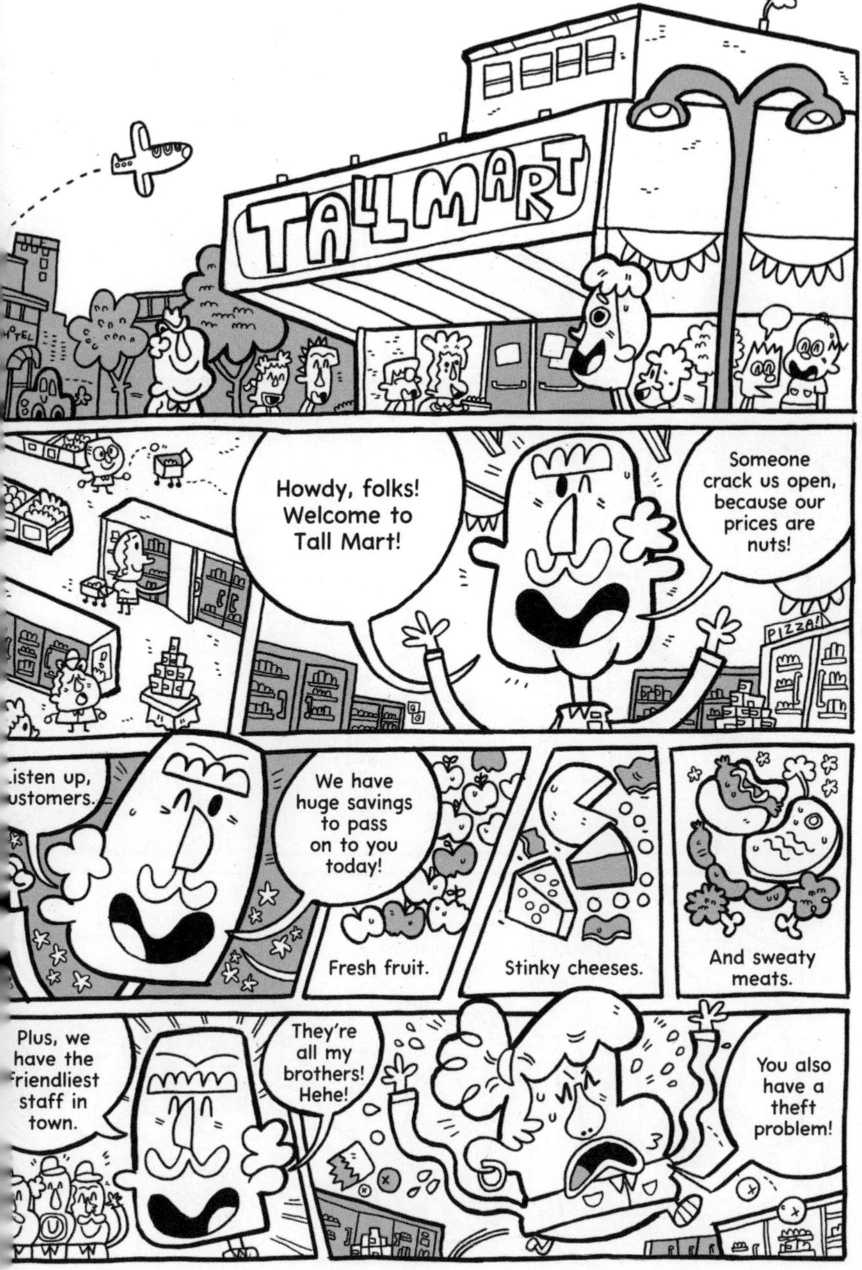
TALLMART
HOTEL
PIZZA!
Howdy, folks! Welcome to Tall Mart!
Someone crack us open, because our prices are nuts!
Listen up, customers.
We have huge savings to pass on to you today!
Fresh fruit.
Stinky cheeses.
And sweaty meats.
Plus, we have the friendliest staff in town.
They're all my brothers! Hehe!
You also have a theft problem!

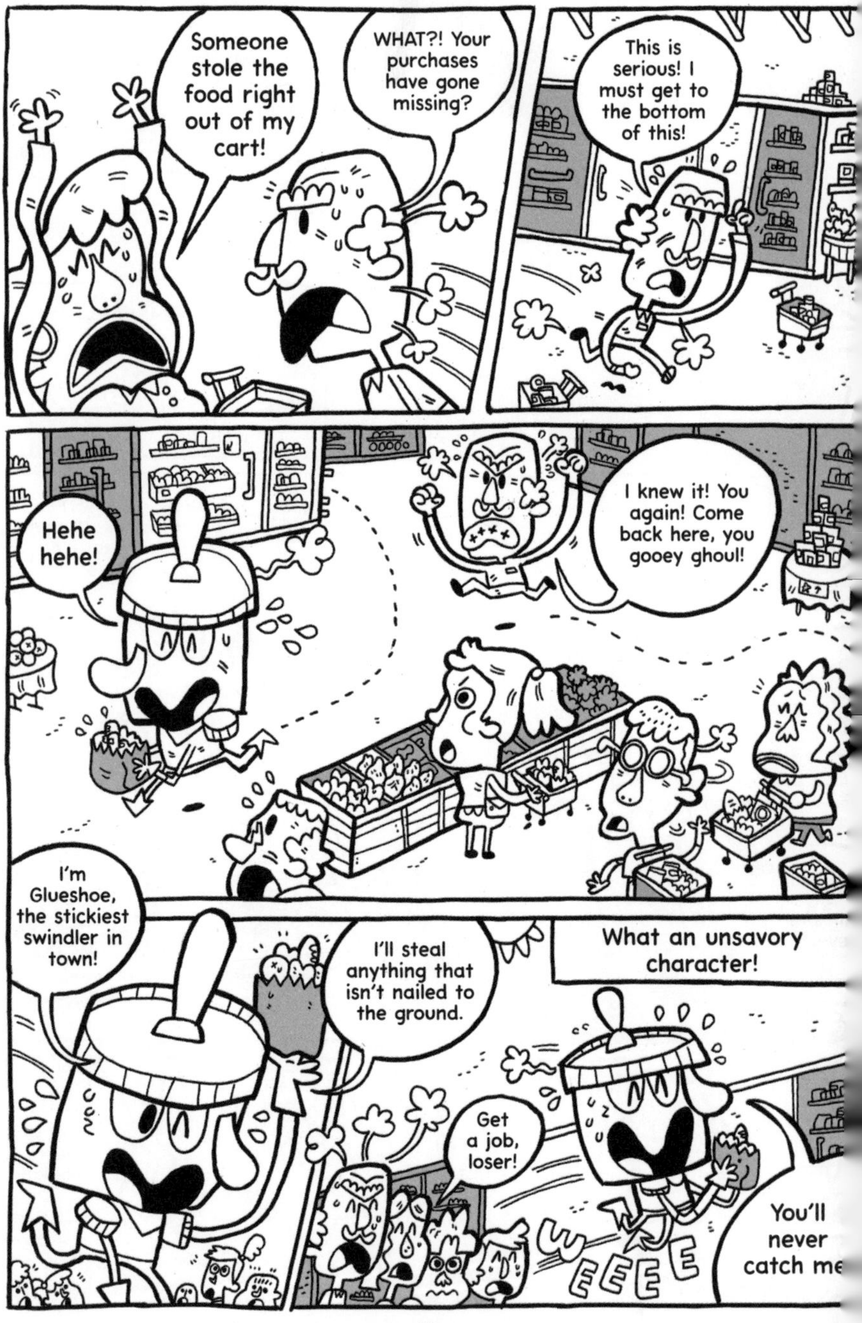
Someone stole the food right out of my cart!
WHAT?! Your purchases have gone missing?
This is serious! I must get to the bottom of this!
Hehe hehe!
I knew it! You again! Come back here, you gooey ghoul!
I'm Glueshoe, the stickiest swindler in town!
I'll steal anything that isn't nailed to the ground.
What an unsavory character!
Get a job, loser!
WEEEE
You'll never catch me

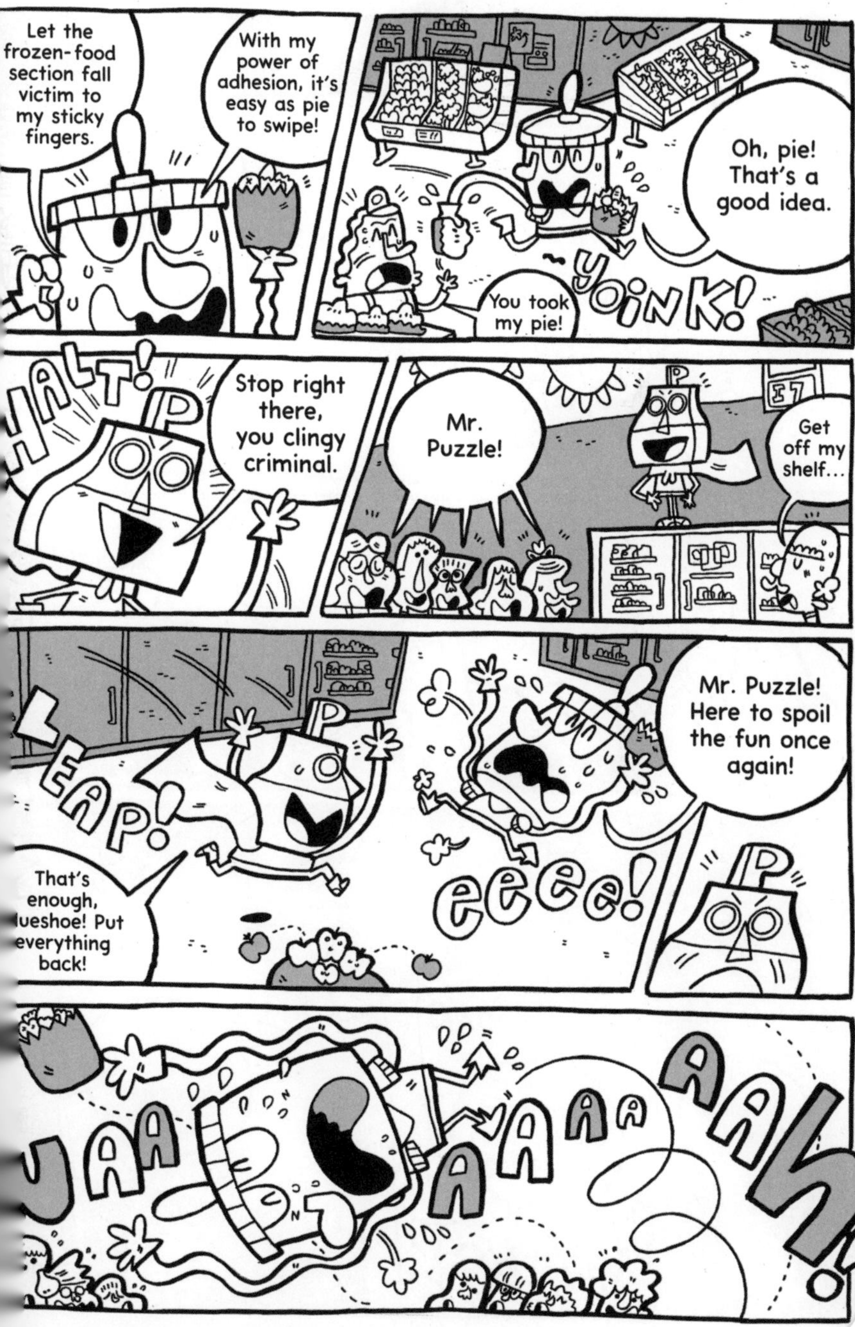
Let the frozen-food section fall victim to my sticky fingers.
With my power of adhesion, it's easy as pie to swipe!
Oh, pie! That's a good idea.
YOINK!
You took my pie!
HALT!
Stop right there, you clingy criminal.
Mr. Puzzle!
Get off my shelf...
LEAP!
That's enough, ueshoe! Put everything back!
eeee!
Mr. Puzzle! Here to spoil the fun once again!
AAAAAAAAAAH!!

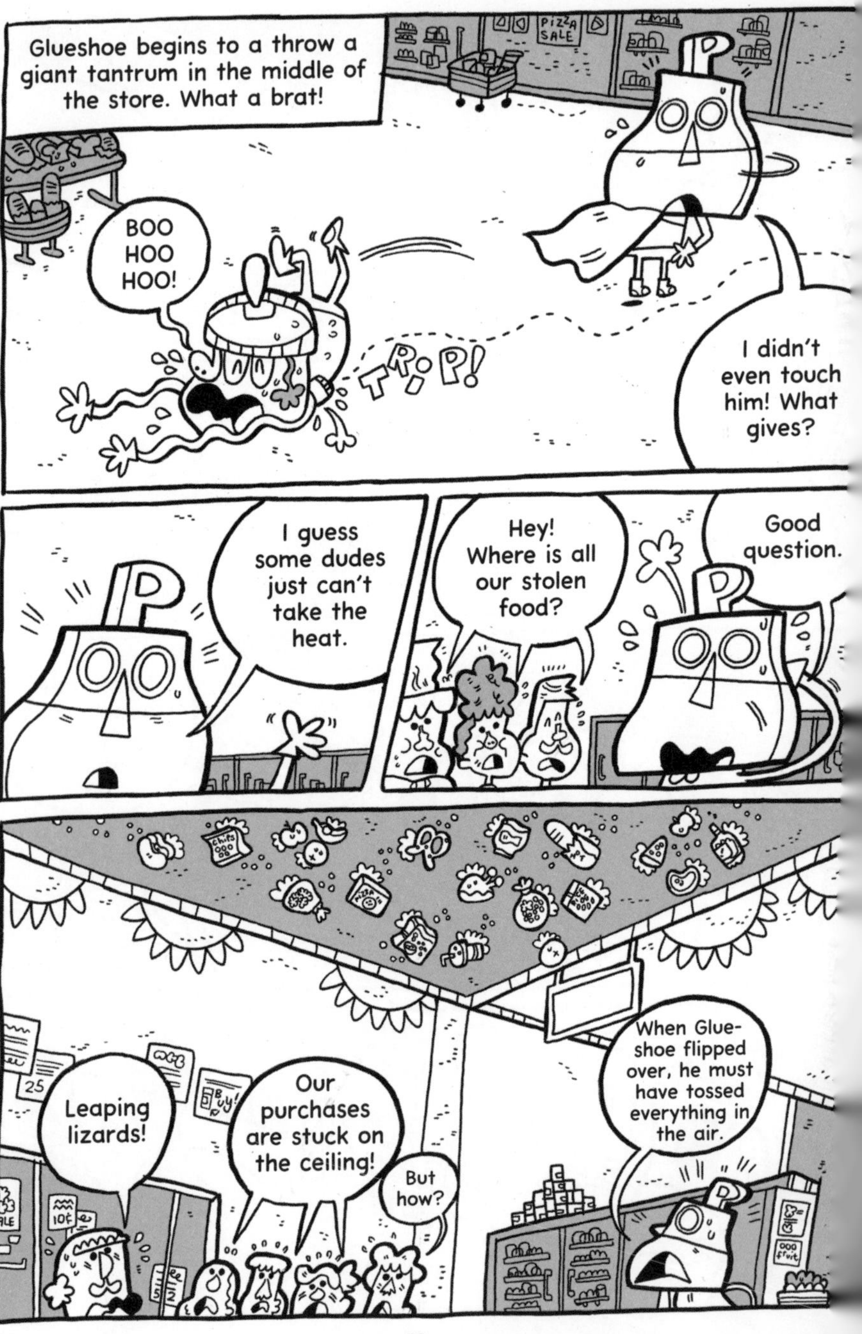
Glueshoe begins to a throw a giant tantrum in the middle of the store. What a brat!
PIZZA SALE
BOO HOO HOO!
TRIP!
I didn't even touch him! What gives?
I guess some dudes just can't take the heat.
Hey! Where is all our stolen food?
Good question.
Leaping lizards!
Our purchases are stuck on the ceiling!
But how?
When Glueshoe flipped over, he must have tossed everything in the air.

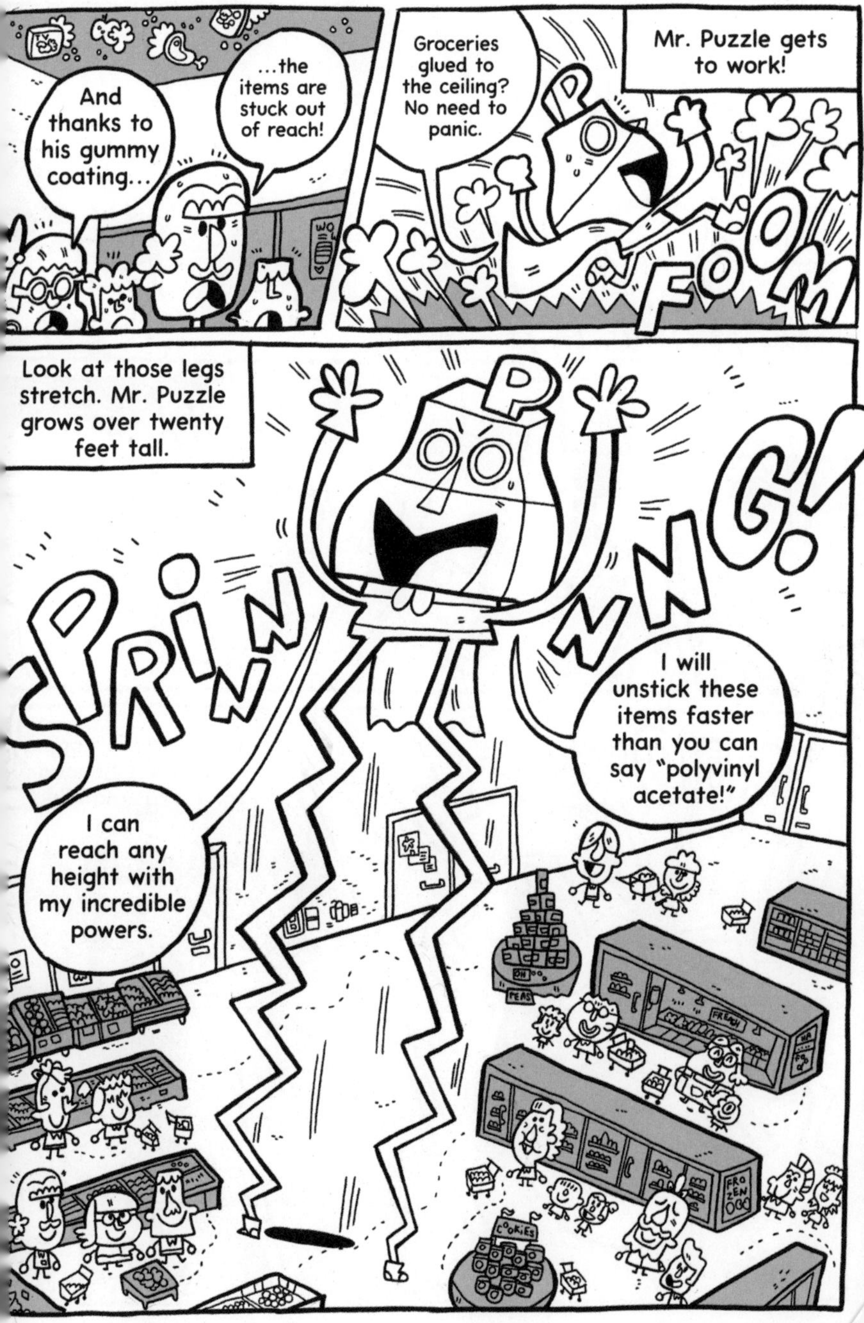
And thanks to his gummy coating...
...the items are stuck out of reach!
Groceries glued to the ceiling? No need to panic.
Mr. Puzzle gets to work!
FOOOM
Look at those legs stretch. Mr. Puzzle grows over twenty feet tall.
SPRINNNNG!
I will unstick these items faster than you can say "polyvinyl acetate!"
I can reach any height with my incredible powers.
PEAS
COOKIES
FROZEN

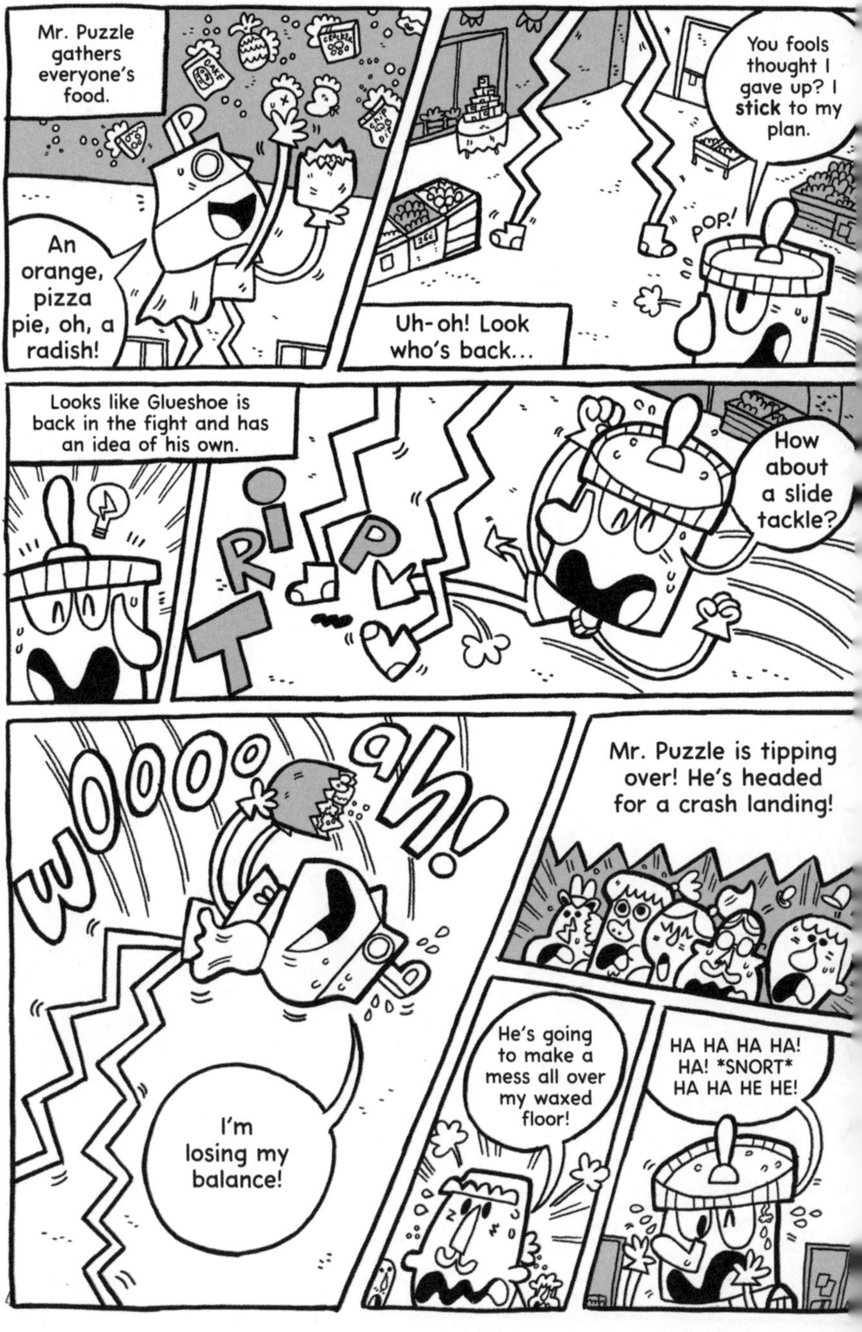
Mr. Puzzle gathers everyone's food.
CAKE
CRACKERS
CHIP DIPS
An orange, pizza pie, oh, a radish!
Uh-oh! Look who's back...
25¢
You fools thought I gave up? I **stick** to my plan.
POP!
Looks like Glueshoe is back in the fight and has an idea of his own.
RIP
How about a slide tackle?
WOOOOah!
I'm losing my balance!
Mr. Puzzle is tipping over! He's headed for a crash landing!
He's going to make a mess all over my waxed floor!
HA HA HA HA! HA! *SNORT* HA HA HE HE!

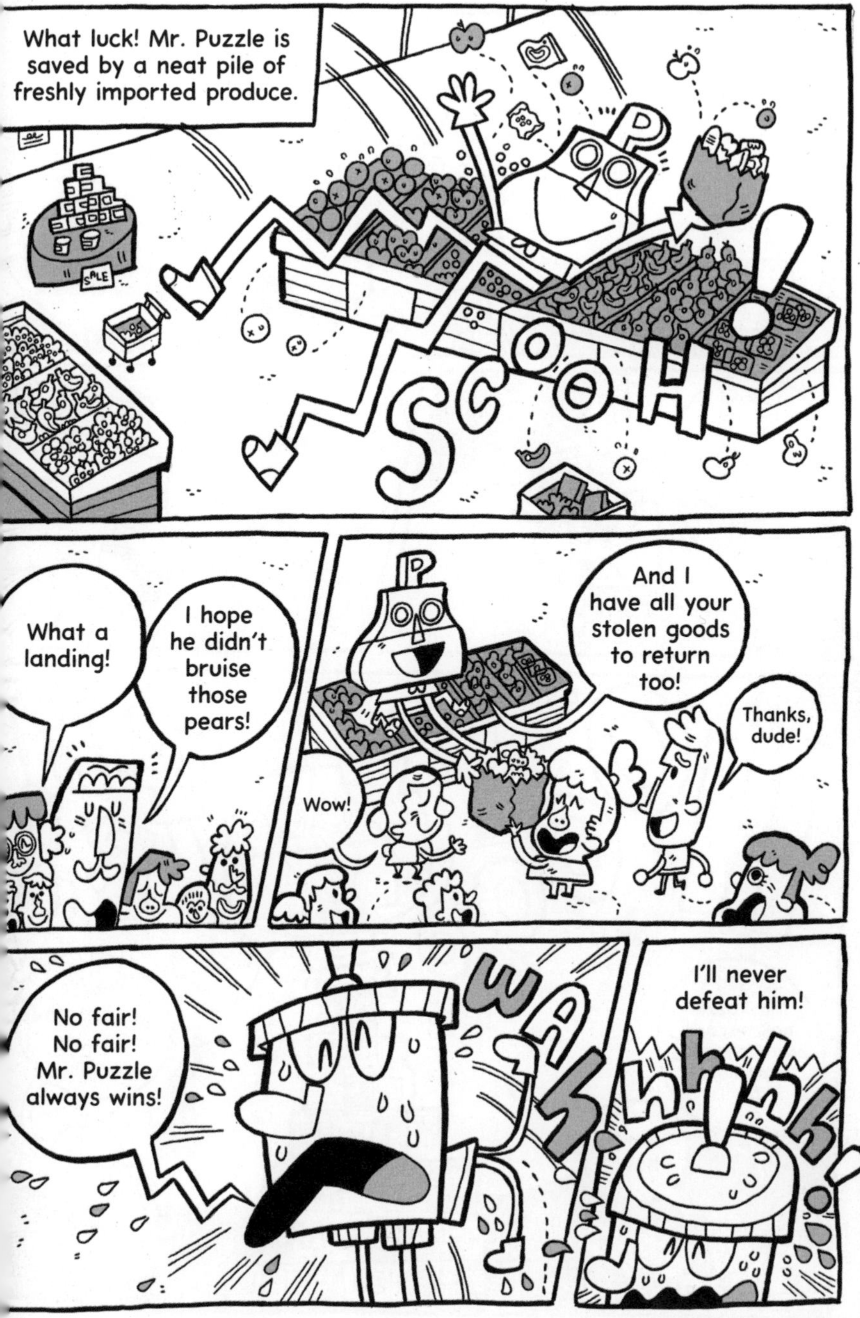
What luck! Mr. Puzzle is saved by a neat pile of freshly imported produce.
SCOOH!
What a landing!
I hope he didn't bruise those pears!
And I have all your stolen goods to return too!
Thanks, dude!
Wow!
No fair! No fair! Mr. Puzzle always wins!
WAAH
I'll never defeat him!
hhhh!

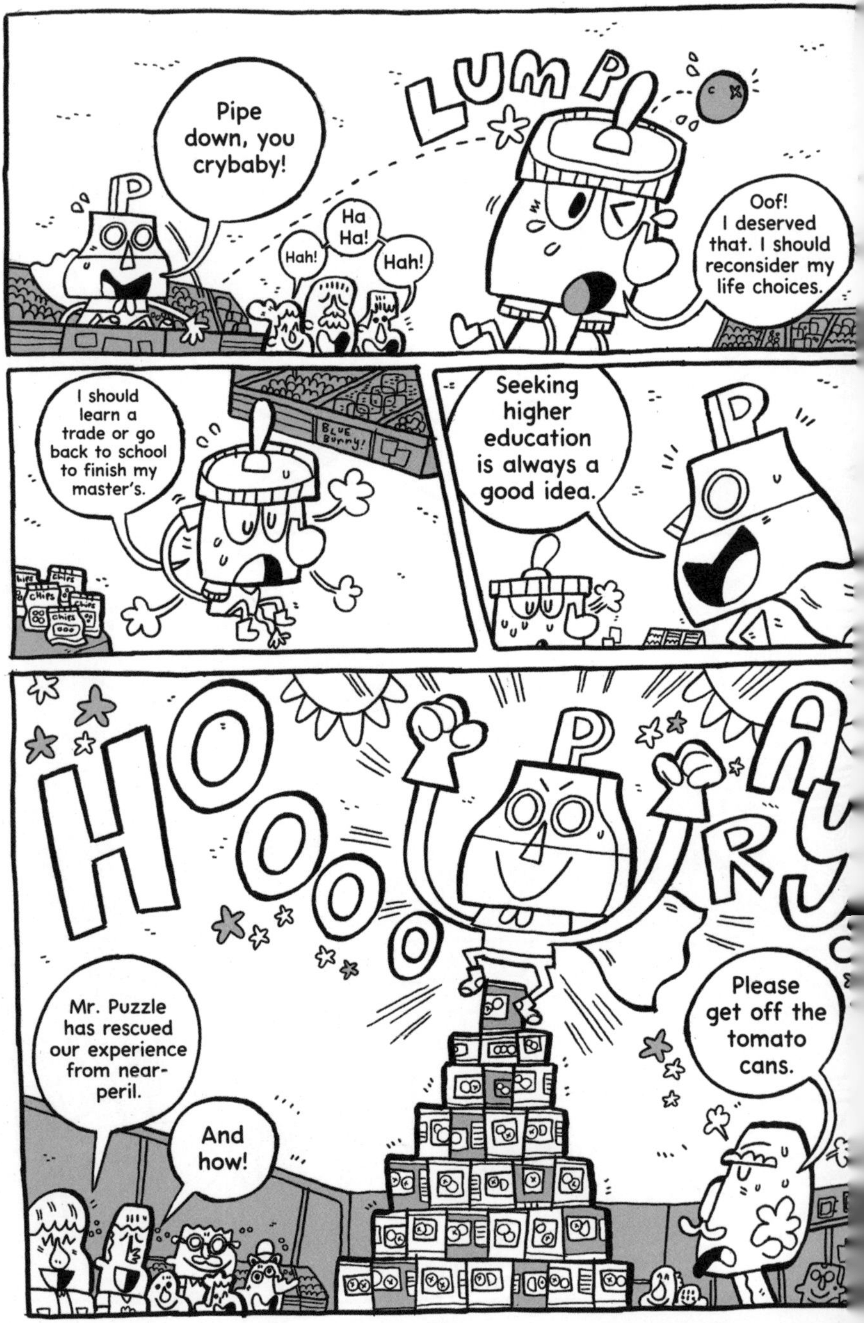
Pipe down, you crybaby!
LUMP
Hah!
Ha Ha!
Hah!
Oof! I deserved that. I should reconsider my life choices.
I should learn a trade or go back to school to finish my master's.
BLUE Bunny!
Seeking higher education is always a good idea.
HOOOOOO
ARRU
Mr. Puzzle has rescued our experience from near-peril.
And how!
Please get off the tomato cans.

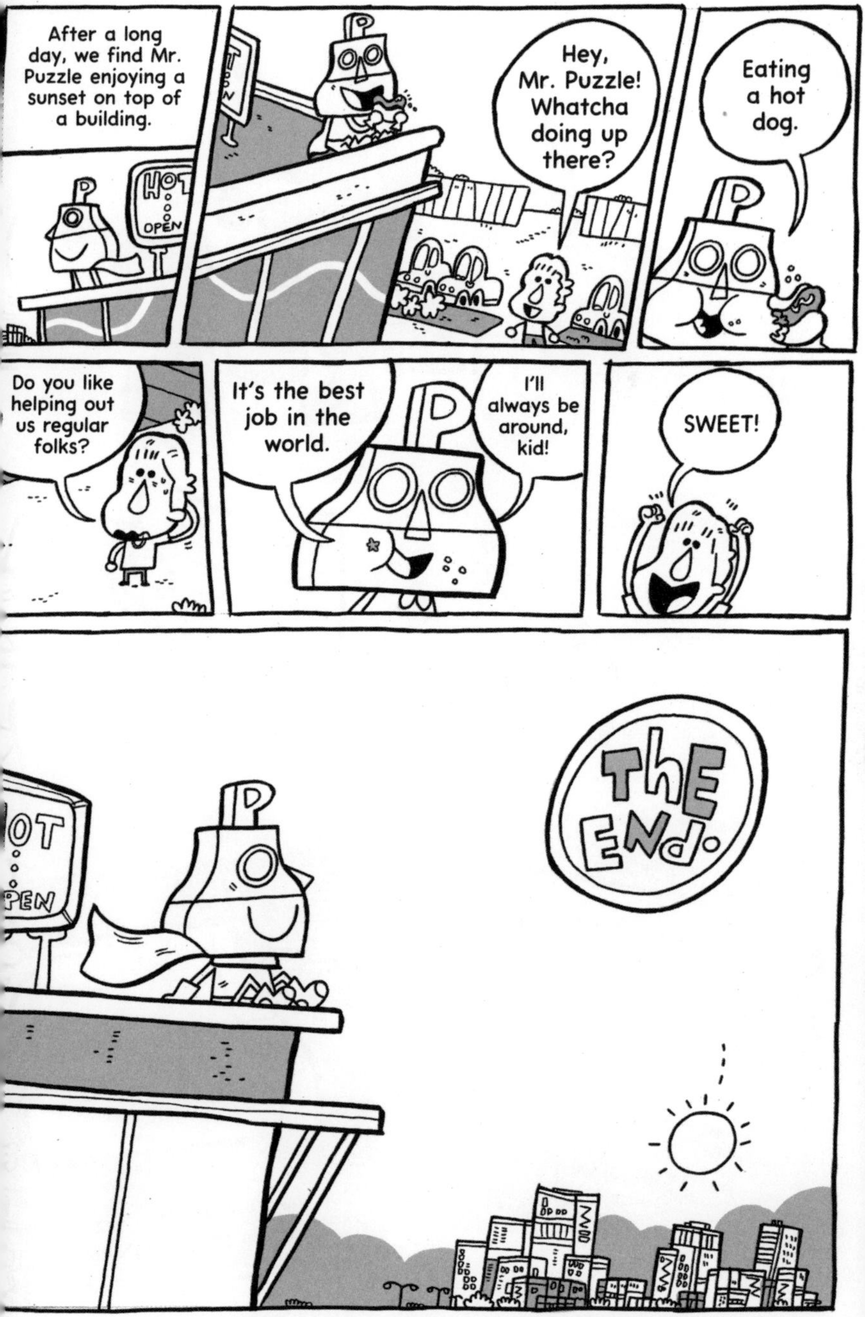
After a long day, we find Mr. Puzzle enjoying a sunset on top of a building.
HOT OPEN
Hey, Mr. Puzzle! Whatcha doing up there?
Eating a hot dog.
Do you like helping out us regular folks?
It's the best job in the world.
I'll always be around, kid!
SWEET!
OT OPEN
THE END.

HOW TO DRAW

You'll need:

 +

A Pencil!    Some Paper!

I.

Draw a shape similar to this.

2.

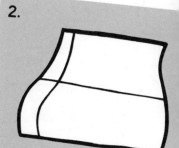

Remember Mr. Puzzle needs some dimension.

3.

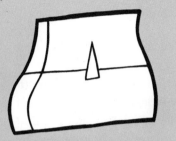

A pointy triangle works great for his nose.

4.

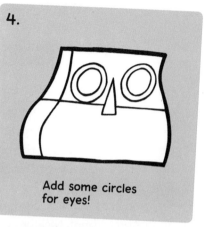

Add some circles for eyes!

5.

Of course he needs a mouth!

6.

We can't forget Mr. Puzzle's "P" and rosy cheeks!

YOU DID IT!

CREATOR

CHRIS ELIOPOULOS is a professional illustrator and cartoonist from Chicago! He is also an adjunct professor at Columbia College Chicago in the art and design department. He is the writer and artist on several all-ages graphic novels and series: *Okie Dokie Donuts* published by Top Shelf; *Gabba Ball!* published by Oni Press; and *Monster Party* published by Koyama Press. Other clients include Disney Animation Studios, Yo Gabba Gabba!, Nick Jr., Cloudkid, and Simon and Schuster.

What has been your favorite part of the book or character to tackle?
CE: I love writing and making up bad guys. They like to shout and let everyone know why they are upset. They all act like two-year-olds with temper tantrums.

Why should people read Mr. Puzzle?
CE: It's a lot of fun, totally silly, and lighthearted. If this comic book were food, it would be a bag of gummy bears.

What's your favorite part about working in comics?
CE: Drawing all day long!

What was the first comic you remember reading?
CE: The Super Mario Adventures inside every issue of *Nintendo Power Magazine*.

Tell us why everyone should read comic books!
CE: What else are you going to read? Furniture assembly instructions or dishwasher owner manuals—yuck!

GLOSSARY

adhesion (ad-HEE-zhuhn)—attachment or stickiness

apparition (ap-uh-RISH-uhn)—another word for ghost

curse (KURSS)—an evil spell intended to harm someone

dean (DEEN)—the senior member of a group

deceive (di-SEEV)—to lie, trick, or mislead

eerie (EER-ee)—strange and frightening

ghastly (GAST-lee)—resembling a ghost

ghoul (GOOL)—an evil being or spirit

logical (LOJ-ih-kuhl)—careful and correct thinking

manic (MAN-ik)—overly enthusiastic or excited

peril (PER-uhl)—danger

pummeled (PUHM-uhl)—pounded or beaten

sludge (SLUHJ)—soft, thick mud

swindler (SWIN-duh-lur)—a person who gets money or property by dishonest means

toxic (TOK-sik)—poisonous

vanquished (VANG-kwishd)—defeated and gained complete control of

MR. PUZZLE
BRAIN BENDERS!

1. Mr. Puzzle got his superpowers from an ancient puzzle. Imagine you are a superhero. Write a paragraph about how you gained superpowers.

Neat!
The puzzle is glowing! Is this supposed to happen?

2. Who is your favorite villain in this book – Heavy E, Professor Clyde, Mucky, or Glueshoe? Explain your answer using examples from the story.

PUSH!

3. In comic books, sound effects (also known as SFX) are used to show sounds. Make a list of all the sound effects in this book, and then write a definition for each term. Soon, you'll have your own SFX dictionary!

4. In comic books, illustrations help tell the story. What is happening in the panels below from page 11? How do you know?

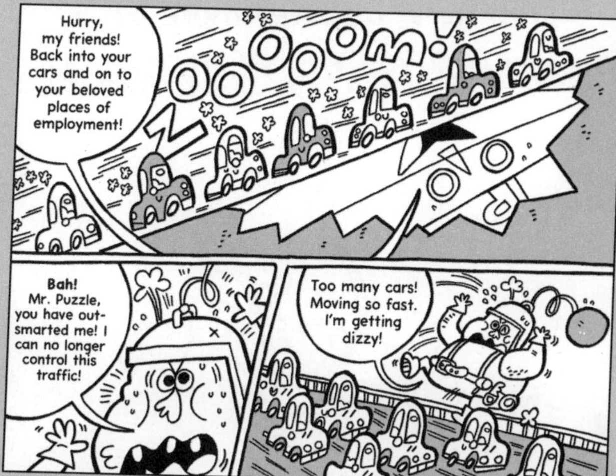
Hurry, my friends! Back into your cars and on to your beloved places of employment!
Bah! Mr. Puzzle, you have outsmarted me! I can no longer control this traffic!
Too many cars! Moving so fast. I'm getting dizzy!

5. On page 17, Mr. Puzzle helps Ivan defeat the evil Professor Clyde. Do you think either of them could have stopped the ghost alone? Why or why not?

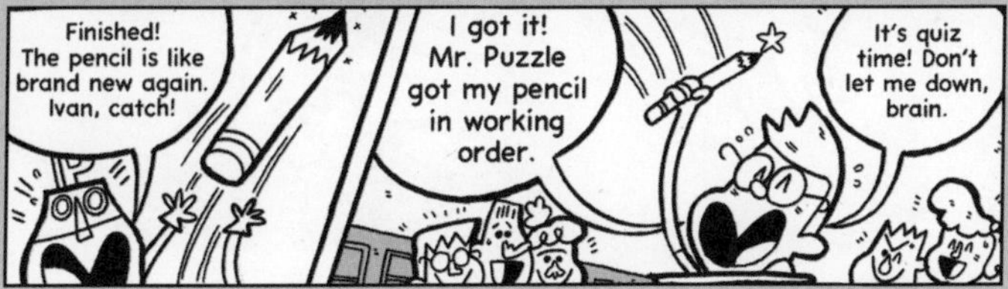
Finished! The pencil is like brand new again. Ivan, catch!
I got it! Mr. Puzzle got my pencil in working order.
It's quiz time! Don't let me down, brain.

6. Write your own Mr. Puzzle adventure! What type of villain will he take on? What superpowers will Mr. Puzzle use to defeat the bad guys? You decide!

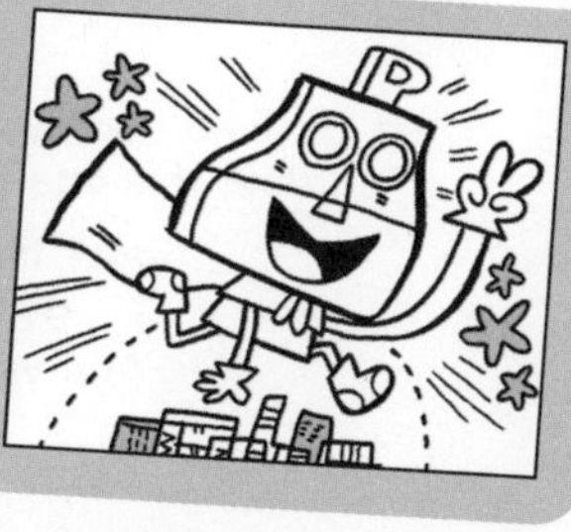

The **Mr. PUZZLE** fun doesn't
stop here! Discover more at...

WWW.CAPSTONEKIDS.COM

Find cool websites and more books
like this one at **www.facthound.com**

Just type in the Book ID:
9781434260246
And you're ready to go!